THUNDER

A Novel of the McCabes

Brad Dennison

Author of
THE LONG TRAIL and SHOSHONE VALLEY

Published by Pine Bookshelf
Buford, Georgia

THE McCABES

The Long Trail
One Man's Shadow
Return of the Gunhawk
Boom Town
Trail Drive
Johnny McCabe
Shoshone Valley
Thunder
Wandering Man

JUBILEE

Preacher With A Gun
Gunhawk Blood (Coming Soon)

THE TEXAS RANGER

Tremain
Wardtown
Jericho (Coming Soon)

Editor and Cover Design: Donna Dennison

Copy Editor: Martha Gulick
                 Loretta Yike

Cover art is from an oil on canvas
By artist James Ward.

To my loving wife and my wonderful children. I would be lost without you.

PART ONE

Range War

1

June, 1882

Johnny McCabe stood on the front porch of the main house. The sun was dropping low in the western sky. Above the valley were long clouds that had been white but were now streaked with crimson.

Johnny had watched darkness fall over the valley from this porch more times than he could ever count over the years. Normally, he had a cup of coffee in one hand and occasionally a glass of scotch.

This time, he held a baby boy who was three weeks old. The boy was swaddled in a blue, flannel blanket.

He held the boy in the crook of his left arm. He kept his right hand free should he have to reach for his gun—old habits die hard.

The door opened behind him and Ginny stepped out. She had a cup of tea in one hand.

He said, "It was nice you and Sam could come out for dinner tonight. It's kind of like old times."

"How many times have we stood on this old porch? Or sat?"

He shrugged. "So many times."

She looked at the baby, and she gave the sort of wondrous grin people do when they look at a baby.

She said, "Little Caleb is already asleep. I had forgotten how good you are with children."

"Here I am, a father again. Most men my age are becoming grandfathers, but I'm here with my newborn son in my arms. I wouldn't change it for the world, though."

She took a sip of tea. "Years ago, not long after we first met, I remember seeing you in a rocker, holding Joshua. He wasn't much older than Caleb. I thought, there's the famed Gunman of the Rio Grande rocking his baby to sleep."

Johnny grinned. "I remember those days."

"So, how long before you, Jessica and the children head back to your cabin?"

"Granny Tate is coming out in a few days to check on Jessica. Make sure everything's all right. Then if she gives her approval, we'll head out."

"I'm glad you brought Jessica here for the delivery."

"Well, there's no wagon road to the canyon. It would be too hard for Granny Tate to get there."

"John, what did you think of her? When she came out for the delivery? She struck me as looking frail."

He nodded. "I don't know how old she is. She was old when she and her family first moved to this area. When was it?"

Ginny thought a moment. "Sixty-eight, I think. Or Sixty-nine."

"She was old then. But she never struck me as frail before. Until recently."

"During the delivery, Haley actually did most of the hands-on work. Granny was observing and advising her."

He nodded. "Haley's learning fast from her. She's going to be a good granny woman."

"Indeed she is. But I don't think Granny could have done the delivery herself."

Johnny looked out at the valley. It was now darker than it had been when Ginny first came out. Funny thing about nightfall, he thought. You can stand and watch it, and it gets darker so gradually you almost don't notice it. But if you look away for a few moments and then look back, you find daylight has slipped away. Sort of like a watched pot never boiling.

He said, "We're all mortal. We pass onward when it's our time. But it's hard to imagine life here without Granny Tate to nurse our ills."

Ginny nodded.

Josh came out from the parlor to join them. He had a glass of scotch in one hand. His hair was pulled back in a tail, and he was in a clean shirt and jeans. He had ridden in for dinner in leather chaps and had been covered with trail dust. Temperance was maintaining the rule Ginny had always enforced—even though this was a working ranch, you washed and wore clean clothes for dinner.

He said, "How's my little brother doing?"

"Fine," Johnny said. "He's asleep. Keep that foghorn voice of yours down, though. I don't want to wake him."

"I *am* being quiet."

Ginny laughed and touched Josh on the arm. "I'll leave you men to talk."

She went back inside.

"So, Pa," Josh said. "I was wondering when you and Jessica and the kids were heading back to the cabin."

He told Josh the same thing he told Ginny.

Josh nodded, and he took a belt of scotch.

Johnny said, "You've got something on your mind."

Josh nodded again. "Temperance doesn't like me to talk business at the dinner table. I suppose she's right. It should be family time. But I have something to ask you."

Johnny said, "Ask away."

"I got a letter on today's stage."

Johnny nodded. A rider had come in from town with the letter.

Josh said, "You know Kirby Jonas? Has a ranch

down in Salmon River country."

Johnny nodded again. "I've met him a couple of times. Runs a good-sized ranch there. About the size of this one."

"Well, he's auctioning off some stock. Must need to raise funds or something. His stock is usually the finest around."

"But you can't go check on it yourself because you're starting spring roundup in a few days."

Josh nodded.

Johnny said, "When's the auction?"

"Eight days. I know you want to get back to the cabin, but it would really help if you could attend that auction."

"Consider it done."

"I really appreciate it. Of course, Jessica and the kids can stay here as long as they need. But you shouldn't be gone long."

"I'll head out tomorrow, to make sure I'm there in plenty of time. If I purchase some stock, the return trip will be a little longer. But either way, I won't be gone long."

Josh nodded. "Thanks, Pa. I hate to put you out this way."

Johnny shook his head. "Nonsense. You run things nowadays and I'm partially retired, but I'm still a part of this ranch."

After it was fully dark, Johnny headed upstairs with Caleb. He climbed the steps carefully, making certain not to jar the baby. Johnny's knees creaked a little, but Caleb slept with a peacefulness that only a baby can muster.

There were four bedrooms on the second floor, and the one that had once held the bunks used by Josh and Dusty now held a queen-sized bed Josh had brought in for his Pa and Jessica to use when they were at the ranch.

The bed filled most of the room, but there was

space between the bed and the wall for something the size of a crib.

Jessica was in bed. Her dark hair had been tied into a braid that was flipped over the front of her shoulder, and she was in a flannel nightgown buttoned to the neck.

"He's asleep," Johnny said.

She was smiling. "Watching the sun go down with his Daddy."

Johnny lowered Caleb into a wooden cradle that was between the bed and the wall. Johnny had built it on rocker slats so it could be rocked from side-to-side. Caleb stirred a bit as Johnny set him down in the cradle but didn't wake up.

Jessica said, "You have such a gentle touch."

Just ahead of the cradle was another one that Johnny had built like the first one. In it was little Elizabeth, sound asleep like her brother.

Johnny said, "Who would have thought we'd have twins?"

"I should have expected it. My grandmother was a twin."

Johnny looked at both children. He said, "Did Lizzy get to sleep all right?"

Jessica had been nursing her while Johnny headed downstairs with Caleb.

She said, "No problems at all."

Johnny stood a moment, looking at Jessica.

She said, "What's wrong?"

"Nothing's wrong, just maybe a little change of plans."

"Like what?"

He told her about the cattle auction.

"I'll be gone three weeks, at the most."

"I just hate to have you gone."

He nodded. "I hate to be away from you and the children."

"And I hate to be an imposition on Josh and Temperance."

"I don't think it's all that much of an imposition. Besides, I'm doing him a big favor."

He unbuckled his gunbelt and slung it over the edge of the bed. He hadn't needed his gun within reach at night for a year now. Maybe some old habits refused to die, but this one was on its way out.

Once his jeans and shirt were off, he climbed into bed.

He said, "Are you all right? If you don't want me to go, I won't."

"No," she said. "It'll be all right. Besides, Granny Tate might not want me going back to the cabin yet, anyway. It's a long ride, and it might be a little while until I'm up to it. Delivering twins is a little more work than delivering one."

"Did I ever tell you you're incredible?"

She gave a big grin. "Not today."

"Not today?"

She laughed. "No sir. Not today, at all. I feel so utterly neglected."

He said, "I'll show you neglect," and gave her a big kiss.

Then they snuggled in under the covers. He was on his side, and she was cuddled in front of him.

He was soon asleep. But she lay there with her eyes open, looking at the dark room around her.

2

Haley had a steak in the skillet, frying it with wild onions she had picked. Jonathan was on the kitchen floor, playing with a set of wooden cowboys and Indians Johnny had carved and given him for Christmas.

Haley's hair was in a bun that was starting to come loose, and stray hairs were flying into her face. She pushed her lower lip out and blew them away. Dang, but the stove was hot. She felt sweat running down along her back and was probably soaking her slip. She would need a long bath, tonight.

The cabin was in a section of pine forest that began at the edge of the grassy valley floor and continued on through the small pass that led out behind the Second Chance. It was built with logs brought down from the ridges. The cabin was a single floor, with a loft up top that would be Jonathan's bedroom once he got a little older.

She heard the horse outside, and went to the window. It was Dusty.

He left his horse at a hitching rail near the back door and came on in. He was in jeans and a range shirt, and his gun was at his side. The gun he had taken from an outlaw years ago, at the little way station in Nevada, when he had come to her rescue.

He always came into the house to get a kiss from Haley and to spend a little time with Jonathan, before he tended to his horse.

He pulled Haley to him and gave her a long kiss. He didn't care about the hair coming loose or the sweat. All he cared about was her.

She said, "I'm so glad you're the wrangler, now. It means you're home every day for supper. Once Josh hires a full-time wrangler, I won't know when to expect you."

He nodded. "It is nice, getting to spend every evening with you and Jon."

Jonathan was wrapping his arms around Dusty's legs and saying, "Daddy!"

Dusty picked him up. "So, how's my favorite man doing?"

He said, "Good, Daddy."

There was a creaking and squealing from out front, and the sound of a horse's hooves on the gravel.

She said, "Sounds like a wagon."

Dusty said, "Wonder who that could be."

Dusty set Jonathan down and went to the front door. Dusty found it was Henry Freeman and Granny Tate.

"Granny," he said with surprise. "Henry. Come on in."

Haley said, "Granny? Is someone sick?"

"No, child," she said. "I just need to talk with you."

Dusty said, "I'll finish supper."

"Thank you," Haley said.

Dusty and Henry went to the kitchen.

"Come on outside," Granny said.

Granny had her cane in one hand. A piece of oak wood that Henry had cut.

Haley noticed Granny was walking carefully, as though she was on ice and didn't want to slip. Haley had seen over the past year that Granny's walking seemed to be getting more precarious.

On the front porch was a long bench Dusty had built out of pinewood. She and Granny sat on it.

Granny said, "I'll get right to the point. You're learnin' to be a granny woman, and you're learnin' right good. But child, you ain't learnin' fast enough."

Granny placed a hand on Haley's. Granny's hand was swollen with arthritis, and it trembled.

Granny said, "Oh, I ain't faultin' you. You're doin' right good. But the thing is, there ain't no easy way to say this."

Haley waited for Granny to say what she had to say.

Granny said, "I'm dyin', child."

"No," Haley said.

Granny nodded. "I know the signs. Believe me. A granny doctor knows these things. I don't think I have a year left. Maybe not even more than a few weeks."

Haley hadn't been expecting to hear something like this. She felt like a wave of ice passed through her, and she shuddered.

"No," she said.

Granny nodded. "It's true."

"There must be something we can do. Your knowledge of herbs and such."

Granny shook her head. "Such things are just the ways of nature, and nothing can change them. We can improve the quality of life, child, but everyone passes on when it's their time."

Haley nodded.

Granny said, "So, this is what we need to do. I have to teach you all that I can, and I don't have much time."

"I go with you on every child-birthing. And any time anyone has a broken bone or the whooping cough."

Granny nodded. "But that ain't enough. We have to start working together every day. I need you at my house every morning, so I can teach you. Every single day. There's a doctor in town and he's good, for what he is, but he doesn't know what I know. I have to pass it on before I'm gone."

Haley thought for a quick moment. "I can have Dusty take Jonathan to the main house. I'm sure Temperance or Bree would watch him."

"Good. Good."

Haley said, "When do you want to start?"

"Tomorrow morning."

3

Josh and Temperance had the main bedroom. The room that had been Pa's when Josh, Jack and Bree had been growing up.

Temperance didn't know what had caused her to wake up, but she realized she was lying awake in the dark room. Josh was on his side, his long hair glowing almost white in the moonlight.

The wind was blowing outside. It rattled the bedroom window. *Coming from an odd direction,* she thought. South or southeast.

Josh had said he thought there was going to be one more snowstorm before summer fully settled in. It was June fourth. Or fifth now, she figured. Must be past midnight. A little late in the year for a snow, but Josh had grown up in these mountains. He would know.

Temperance listened, to see if Cora was calling to her. Maybe that was why she had woken up. Or maybe one of the twins was crying.

But everything was quiet. As it should be.

Then she heard footsteps in the corridor outside the bedroom door. She barely heard them. Light steps that made almost no sound, except for the floorboards creaking.

It couldn't be Pa, she thought. He was often up in the night, checking the place to make sure it was safe. But he had a heavier way of stepping and made the floorboards creak more. Temperance figured it was either Bree or Jessica.

Probably heading down to the outhouse. Temperance had heard that in some of the well-to-do homes in New York or Boston, or out in San Francisco, water closets were being installed. An indoor outhouse, with running water. She couldn't imagine such a thing.

She waited and listened, but neither door opened.

Both doors, the front door and the one in the

kitchen, had a squeal to their hinges. Pa had never fixed them because he said he wanted to be able to hear when a door opened at night. Now that Pa and Jessica had moved to the cabin and were only here occasionally, Josh had asked her if she wanted those hinges greased.

No, she had said. *If Pa thought it was a good idea not to, then maybe we shouldn't.*

She decided to get up and see what was going on. No need to wake up Josh. It wasn't like there was going to be a gunfight, or anything.

She slipped on her housecoat, tied the front and stepped into slippers.

No one used a lantern to get around in this house. When she had first moved into the family house four years ago, she had found it a little strange, but Pa had his reason.

He had said if you have a lantern in your hand, then anyone outside could tell where you were by watching the windows light up as you passed by. Aunt Ginny had said Pa lived in a state of war. Always ready for shots to be fired. Temperence doubted shots would be fired, but even still, she stepped out into the dark hallway without a lantern.

As she took the stairs down to the parlor, she could see a lamp was on in the kitchen.

She found Jessica building a fire in the stove.

"Jess," she said. "What're you doing up at this hour? It has to be..,"

The clock on the mantel chimed twice.

"It has to be two o'clock." She laughed.

Jessica grinned. "I just couldn't sleep. I thought I might make some tea."

"I can make the fire."

"Thanks. But I feel like doing something. Being on my feet for a change."

Once the fire was going, Jessica filled a kettle of water from the kitchen pump.

Temperance said, "At least let me carry that. I don't want to get Granny Tate mad at me."

Jessica grinned and gave in.

Temperance set the kettle on the stove and they sat at the table to wait for the water.

Jessica said, "You don't have to sit up with me. I know tomorrow comes early."

"No, I'm not feeling tired. The thought of some tea sounds good."

They chatted while the water heated. Jessica commented on how good dinner had been. Mister Chen in town had shown Temperance how to stir fry some roots and mushrooms, and she had served it with beef and onions for the evening's dinner.

Then Jessica said, "You know what I would really like? A glass of wine. But I can't. It would get into the baby's milk."

Temperance said, "What's troubling you, Jess?"

Jessica let out a long sigh. "This trip Johnny's going to take, for the cattle auction. I can't get it out of my mind."

"I hope you don't feel you're any kind of imposition, being here. The way we see it, the house belongs to all of us. Josh and I just manage it."

"I appreciate that. But I just don't like Johnny being away. I have a bad feeling about this, and I just can't shake it. The feeling that something bad is going to happen. That this might be the time he doesn't come back at all."

4

Temperance didn't know what to think. So she said, "I'm sure he'll be fine. He always has been."

Jessica said, "Aunt Ginny has said one of the hardest things is waiting for these men to come home from their various journeys. And someday, you and I both know, one of them won't be coming home."

Temperance gave a reluctant nod of the head. "I've thought about that, even though I try not to."

The tea kettle eventually began whistling. Temperance poured hot water into a tea pot, dropped in a tea ball filled with Earl Gray and brought it over to the table. Jessica fetched two sets of cups and saucers.

Temperance said, "Maybe he shouldn't go."

"But then Josh will want to go. He has to be here for the roundup."

"True."

Jessica said, "Maybe I'm just being foolish. Maybe it's just late, and I'm still recovering from the delivery. And Granny Tate has said sometimes women feel down in the dumps after a delivery. I didn't with Cora, but that doesn't mean I'm not now."

Temperance shrugged and smiled. "Maybe that's it."

Temperance was awake before sunrise. Life started early on the ranch—Jessica had said it, herself. Once she was dressed and had her hair in a bun, she went out and collected the eggs, and had a fire in the stove and coffee boiling. All before the sun began peeking over the horizon.

Pa came down the stairs with his bedroll and saddle bags. "Figured I'd get an early start," he said. "Dusty's not here yet, so I'll go saddle Thunder myself."

"Thunder can wait," she said. "You need a good breakfast before you leave."

She served up eggs and steak. Josh came in from splitting some wood and he filled the wood box.

He said, "I got Thunder saddled for you."

"Thanks, son."

"Wasn't easy. That horse can be ornery."

Johnny grinned.

Temperance said, "How's Jessica this morning?"

Johnny washed down a mouthful of steak with a splash of coffee. "I woke her up to say goodbye, but she's probably asleep again. She had trouble sleeping last night."

Do tell, Temperence thought.

Once breakfast was gone, Johnny pulled on his jacket. It was a faded brown, and waist-length. The same jacket he had been wearing when Temperence was first introduced to the family.

Johnny headed outside with his bedroll under one arm and his saddlebags over his shoulder, and his rifle in one hand. Josh and Temperance followed him out. Bree was there, too.

Bree said, "I didn't want you to leave before I could get a hug."

She got her hug, then Johnny slid the rifle into the saddle and tied the saddlebags and bedroll to the back of his saddle.

Josh said, "I really appreciate you doing this, Pa."

"No trouble at all."

They shook hands, and Josh said, "Ride safe."

Temperance got a hug, then Johnny said to Thunder, "So, old friend, you ready for one more ride?"

The horse didn't answer, of course, but somehow Temperance thought Thunder understood him.

Pa swung up and into the saddle. "All right. I'll see you all in three weeks, or sooner."

Thunder was only half-broken and particular. He didn't like the feeling of spurs.

Johnny reached to the side of the horse's neck with his right hand and gave Thunder a couple of taps. "Let's ride."

The horse started forward. Johnny turned Thunder down the trail that would take him to the wooden bridge and beyond. But he didn't do it with the reins. Thunder didn't like them either, and he didn't always respond well. Johnny got him to change direction by touching one knee to Thunder's shoulder.

Temperance figured Johnny had a coffee pot and a bag of coffee stuffed into his saddle bags, and a box of cartridges for his pistol and another for his rifle. Some matches, and probably a skillet. But no food. He would shoot his supper as he traveled.

She doubted he would take trails. He would travel straight through the mountains, taking as direct a route as possible. Sleep under the stars beside a campfire.

Somehow, it seemed natural. This man, whom she sometimes thought of as one of the last of the mountain men.

Temperance turned and looked up at the window, because the bedroom Pa and Jessica now used when they were here overlooked the front yard.

She saw Jessica in the window, looking off toward the bridge, watching Johnny ride away.

Temperance knew the bad feeling Jessica had the night before hadn't left her.

Temperance looked back to the trail. Pa was now beyond the wooden bridge.

Ride safe, Pa, she said to herself. *Come back to us.*

5

Bree and Charles rode up the slope of the ridge they
called McCabe Mountain. They were surrounded by
pines that stood tall, with trunks as straight as arrows.

Charles said, "I hope to get started on our cabin,
once spring roundup is done."

The last couple of weeks had been warm, and
Bree could smell spring on the air. The snow was gone
from all except the taller mountains. Josh said they had
at least one more snowfall coming, possibly two, but
Bree wasn't going to think about that now. She was
going to enjoy the day.

She had a dark brown braid that fell down the
length of her back. She was in a gray Boss of the Plains
hat and a waist-length jacket. She wore canvas
trousers, something girls back East or in San Francisco
would not normally want to be caught dead in, but Bree
had little interest in fashion sense. When you're riding
in the mountains, you dress for function. Her Colt was
holstered at her right hip.

Charles said, "I still can't believe you shot and
killed a full-grown grizzly when you were only ten."

She nodded. "Sure did. Why's that so hard to
believe?"

"Well," he said. "It's just that most girls of ten are
playing with dolls, not out shooting grizzlies."

She smiled. "Most girls aren't the daughter of
Johnny McCabe."

He returned the smile. "So very true. And I'm
learning I really shouldn't be surprised at anything you
do. You are your father's daughter."

Charles was in a wide-brimmed hat, and he wore
a vest to hold his wallet while he rode. He was in tall
riding boots, and a pistol was holstered on his left side,
turned backwards for a cross-draw. A bandana was tied

loosely about his neck.

It was a Wednesday, normally a work day, but at dinner the night before, talk had turned to the grizzly Bree had shot when she was ten. She wanted to take Charles out to the ridges to show him where it had happened. She wanted Charles to have the day off.

Josh said, "Has anyone ever said *no* to you?"

"They've tried. Hasn't worked so far."

So here she and Charles were, on what would normally be a workday, riding up the side of McCabe Mountain.

She reined up. "Right here is where it happened. I think. It's been nine years. The land changes."

"So, what were you doing up here alone?"

"Tryin' to find Josh. He had gotten himself trapped in that old mining shaft where we're building our new cabin. Pa has boarded up the shaft but good. Back then, we didn't know about the shaft until Josh stepped onto the rotting boards covering it, and down he went. Nothing he likes to talk about today, especially because it was his kid sister who come along and rescued him."

Charles was chuckling.

She said, "I was on Midnight."

She was today, too. A black mustang Pa had caught in the mountains, years ago.

She said, "The grizzly had charged at Josh the day before, and he grazed it deep on one shoulder. We don't know why the bear tried to attack him."

"Grizzlies normally won't attack, but they can be unpredictable."

"Sure can. This one had blood on its shoulder, and when it saw me, it went up on its hind legs. I had my rifle with me," she tapped the yellow-boy Winchester on her scabbard down by her left leg. "Back then, Pa loaded it with less powder, so it wouldn't have as much of a kick. I pulled the rifle and took aim and brought the bear down with one shot."

Charles sidled his horse up to hers.

He said, "You're the stuff of legend yourself, you know."

She beamed a smile.

He said, "And I count myself as one of the few who have ever kissed a legend."

He leaned over, she leaned into him, and their lips met.

Then Midnight shifted away and Bree had to grab the saddle horn and push down hard into one stirrup to keep from falling.

She laughed. "I guess Midnight's not a romantic."

6

Old Ches was out behind the barn, getting the chuck wagon ready.

Josh walked on over. He was in his leather chaps and had a bandana tied around his neck.

He said, "I'm going to ride out and have a final look at the grass before we start the roundup. How're things going with the chuck wagon?"

Ches said, "It took a beating last summer, on the trail drive. But I'll have it ready."

Ches had hair that was snow white, and he was a little bent at the shoulders. He had lost some teeth over the years, and his skin was leathery.

Josh said, "Ches, how are old are you?"

Ches shrugged. "Don't rightly know. Lost count a long time ago. I remember when James Monroe was president, so I've gotta be over seventy."

"Most men your age have retired long ago."

"Not me," Ches said. "Can you see me retired? What would I do with myself? Sit on a front porch in a rocker all day? I got too much livin' left to do."

Josh grinned and nodded his head. He was funning Ches, anyway. Ches was one of those men who got older, but never seemed to grow old. That man in town was like that, too. Mister Chen. Josh hoped to one day join that club. He couldn't see himself retiring, either.

Ches said, "You think the weather'll hold up for a roundup?"

Josh glanced skyward. It was mostly blue, but there was a layer of white clouds off to the west.

He said, "They're gonna have some snow in the mountains tonight or maybe tomorrow. I bet Pa's gonna see some on his way to the Jonas ranch. But we should be all right."

Josh saddled up Rabbit and headed out. He told

Temperance he expected to be home for supper.

He turned Rabbit east, and through the pass that would lead him out of the valley, to the grassy hills beyond.

He didn't plan on riding all the way to the line cabin. His plan was mainly to check range conditions. They were three days away from starting the round-up, and he needed to be picking a location for the camp and which part of the range they would be using.

Once he was beyond the valley, he dismounted and loosened the cinch so Rabbit could breathe a little. Josh was about five miles west of the line cabin. A few more miles southeast would bring him to a small ranching community that was starting to be called Harlowton.

The breeze was cool, and he was in a jacket. The nights were still downright cold, but he expected to be back at the main house before then.

He thought he might ride north for a while. There was a stream that had always been the unofficial border between McCabe range and Willbury range. Pa had laid official claim to the southern end of the valley and the ridges around it and the stretch of range that went out to the line cabin beyond the valley. Tom Willbury had laid similar claim to a patch of land further north. A small river served as the unofficial boundary between the two.

The river was fed from streams and springs in the mountains, and over the winter, a rock slide had altered the flow of it. The river now cut south into the section of range used by the McCabe herd. Josh wanted to see what condition this section of range would be in. He was concerned the stream would be flooding low-lying areas and making the range unusable.

He found the stream flowing strong with spring run-off, which it usually was this time of year. The stream was spilling over the grass but was already conforming to the shape of the land, creating what would develop into a new streambed. Like with most young streams, it was shallow and wide, and running fast.

He let Rabbit drink a little, and even cupped his hands to take a drink himself. The water was cold, but a little gritty. The stream was still washing up bits of gravel over its new water course.

He decided to ride on. The unofficial border was the former streambed. He wanted to see what the grass looked like in that area, now that it was being deprived of the stream.

He passed some longhorns, grazing on winter grass, and new green springtime grass where they could find it.

He noticed the brand on one was on the left shoulder. A *W*, slanted like it had been caught in the wind. The Flying W. Tom Willbury's brand. Not unusual, he knew. Longhorns didn't tend to respect boundaries, and roamed where they pleased. McCabe riders often found Flying W cattle on this side of the boundary, and Tom found Circle M and Circle T cattle on his side. Such critters were usually just escorted back to the proper range.

As Josh rode along, he saw eight longhorns chewing away on grass, and a couple looked up at him lazily. Josh turned Rabbit over toward them. Two scattered but the rest didn't bother. A quick glance showed him that five of them had the Flying W brand. The other three were turned at a wrong angle and he couldn't see their brands.

He continued on and found the old streambed about two miles from where the new stream was running. It was wide and sandy, and completely dry. It sunk about three feet below the sod, because it had been running a lot of years. It twisted and turned, the way an old streambed will.

There was a small ravine ahead, and the dry streambed ran through the middle of it. Dug out by the stream, over time. Two sections of bedrock jutted out, and rose to maybe eight feet above the sod. They stood a hundred feet apart. Josh had started calling them the *Twin Sisters* years ago, and the name had caught on.

His brother Jack figured during the last ice age, glaciers had dug their way across the land and exposed the sections of bedrock. Prior to that, the Twin Sisters had probably been a number of feet underground. Jack, the scholar. Josh didn't know about such things and had little interest. His main concern was finding good grass.

He turned Rabbit toward the Sisters. He figured he would let Rabbit graze a bit, while he climbed one rock for a look around. He reined up by one of the Sisters and swung out of the saddle.

A gun was fired from somewhere behind him. The bullet caught the rock just beyond him and knocked off a small chunk of it.

Josh ran toward the rock and dove for cover behind it. Rabbit went charging off.

Josh drew his pistol, and waited. Where had the gun been fired from? This land was wide open, with a small grassy rise maybe five miles to the west. The only place of concealment would be the other Sister.

Josh took a chance and peered around the edge of the rock. The gun was fired again, and the bullet took off another chip of rock. Josh ducked back.

The gunman was indeed behind the other Sister. He had apparently been hiding there as Josh rode up.

An odd place for a highwayman, Josh thought. There was no trail out here. You could hide in a place like that and wait weeks and see no other riders.

But the first order of business was stopping the gunman, before one of his bullets could find Josh.

The gunman fired again. Bullets ricocheted against the rock, and sparks shot away.

Josh realized from the sound of the gunshots that there were two guns being used. One sounded like a rifle. Maybe a Winchester .44 caliber. The other was a pistol. A .44 or a .45. They sounded a little different. A rifle had more of a full-throated sound.

He decided they were trying to goad him into firing back and wasting ammunition. He wasn't going to bite.

Instead, he looked at the back side of the Sister he was using for cover. It was rough and uneven, but it looked like there were some usable handholds and footholds.

Josh slid his pistol back into the holster, then started to climb.

The rock was rough and jagged, and he scraped one finger. A boot sole slipped but he hung on and continued up.

Once he was on top, he dropped flat so he wouldn't be skylined, and drew his gun again.

He couldn't see the gunmen from here, but he didn't think they saw him either, because they fired again at the lower part of the rock. Still trying to goad him into firing back.

He waited. Maybe they would think he was wounded. Maybe not. But sooner or later they had to move, and he would have a good shot at them from up here.

The sun was warm, but the breeze was a little chilly. Such could be expected this time of year.

Then he saw movement. They were coming. Two men, both in wide-brimmed hats. One was indeed holding a rifle, and the other a revolver.

They approached the rock carefully, like they weren't sure.

That was when Josh stood up to full height and cocked his revolver.

"Don't move, gentlemen, or you're dead."

They looked up at him, but they didn't try to fire.

Josh had them throw their guns aside, and then lie face-down in the grass while he climbed down. He figured they didn't have time to get to their feet and run to their guns, but he found they didn't even try.

Josh allowed them to rise as far as their knees.

"You a McCabe?" one of them said. He was about

thirty and needed a shave. The other was younger, maybe late teens.

"I'm asking the questions," Josh said. "Just who might you be?"

"Ain't sayin'."

Josh shook his head. "All I have to do is go over to where your horses must be, behind that rock. Check their brands."

"All right. We ride for the Willburys."

"Since when does Tom Willbury shoot at men on McCabe range?"

The older one shrugged. "Don't know. We was just hired to stop anyone trespassin' on Willbury land."

This had Josh a little puzzled. "But this isn't Willbury land. We're on the McCabe side of the streambed."

"We was told to shoot anyone who's north of the stream that's south of here."

Now Josh was really puzzled.

He glanced up toward the sun, to gauge the time. It was approaching noon. Good, he thought. Plenty of daylight left. Because he had a lot of riding ahead of him.

He said to the two on their knees. "Now, pull your boots off. You're going back to the Willbury ranch, but you're going back in your socks. And with no guns."

"Aw, mister," the young one said.

Josh said, "You're lucky you're not going back draped over the back of a horse. Now get those boots off."

7

Dusty was in the corral watching one of the mustangs run. A buckskin colored horse that Bree had named Buckskin. The horse had taken a tumble with Kennedy on it a week ago and injured a leg. But now the horse seemed to be moving around well enough.

Kennedy came over. A man with a wide-brimmed black hat, long dark hair and a handlebar mustache.

He said, "How long do you think it'll be before that horse'll be ready to ride?"

Dusty's hat was hanging along his back from the chinstrap. He was standing inside the corral and leaning one elbow against the top rail.

He said, "He looks fine, but I'd like to wait another week. Err on the side of caution."

Kennedy nodded. "This one's my favorite cutting horse. I'm glad he's gonna be all right."

Haley had come out with Granny Tate to look at Kennedy after the fall. He had separated his left shoulder in the fall. Granny Tate had him grab a chair with one arm, and told Haley to push down on the top of the shoulder. Haley did. The shoulder went back into place, but Kennedy said it hurt worse than the fall did.

Granny had grinned. "Always seems to."

Dusty said, "How's your shoulder?"

"Not bad. It's comin' along."

"Good. Josh is talking about starting the round-up in three days. We need all our hands in top condition."

"I'll be all right. I use my rope with my right, not my left."

Dusty wished he would be working the roundup alongside Kennedy and the others, instead of serving as wrangler. Overseeing the McCabe remuda was not an easy job. Fred Mitchum had made it look easy, and Dusty wished old Fred was here, now.

Part of serving on this ranch meant doing some farrier work. Shoeing needed to be done. Buckskin had thrown a shoe when he had fallen. Dusty had been reluctant to nail a shoe on until he knew the leg wasn't sprained. Two others had thrown shoes, too.

Once Dusty had the anvil and bellows set up in front of the barn, he tied a leather apron on over his jeans.

He was about to go fetch Buckskin when he heard the drumming of hooves on the wooden bridge. A rider was coming up the trail, and he was moving fast.

Dusty stepped around the barn so he would have a better look at the trail, and he saw it was Josh. Rabbit wasn't at a full gallop, but he was halfway there.

Josh brought Rabbit to a sliding stop in front of Dusty. Rabbit was lathered, and he pranced a bit. Rabbit had been ridden hard, but he loved to run and wanted to go some more.

Dusty said, "Didn't expect you back till nightfall."

"I was shot at." Josh swung out of the saddle.

"Shot at?"

"Two yahoos out by the Twin Sisters. They were waiting for riders."

Dusty blinked with surprise. "What were they doing out there?"

"We're about to find out. I want a fresh horse saddled." Josh said. His dander was up, which Dusty had found wasn't all that difficult a thing to achieve. Josh was talking fast and with words that were hard and clipped. "And one for you, too. You're coming with me. And Charles. Where is he?"

"Still off riding with Bree."

Josh gave an impatient nod. "That's right. He's got the day off. Well, it's just you and me, then."

"Where are we going?"

"The Willbury ranch."

"What do you need me for?"

"To make sure I don't kill someone."

8

The Willbury ranch house was on a grassy section of land a two-hour ride north of the town of Jubilee. The house had begun as a cabin, made of logs Tom Willbury had cut himself and hauled from a ridge nearly a mile away. That had been only a few years after the McCabes had settled in, further south. The house was still a single level, but it had sprawled over the years. And the entire building was still made of logs.

Thomas Hezekiah Willbury, Jr., the first born of Tom, was called Kye as a shortened version of his middle name. He was twenty-four years old and he was doing his level best to run this place. Ever since his Paw had gotten injured and couldn't run the place anymore.

Kye was tall and thin, with high cheekbones and overly pronounced lips. Freckles decorated his cheeks, and he had a shock of red hair that kept falling along his brow.

He stood in the great room, looking at a longhorn rack eight feet wide that was mounted over the mantel of a hearth made of stones. Kye reached up to push back the shock of hair for the hundredth time today.

He felt like he was only a fraction of the man his father was. His father was built like a bull. Kye had seen his dad wrestle down the very steer whose horns were now mounted over the mantel. He had seen his father bend a horseshoe with his bare hands.

And now the man was in bed, his eyes shut. He hadn't opened his eyes or spoken a word in months.

Tom Willbury was the greatest man Kye had ever seen. They had been in a gunfight with rustlers three years earlier, and Tom had taken a bullet to the shoulder but kept on shooting. Kye had seen his father hold his own in an arm wrestling contest with Hunter, down in Jubilee. There weren't many men who could do that.

But the previous autumn, about a month before Thanksgiving, Tom Willbury had fallen from a horse. He landed hard and just didn't get up. Kye figured his father had hit his head on a rock.

Knocked cold, Kye figured. Kye and a couple of cowhands got the senior Willbury back to the house. Hours passed, but he didn't wake up.

Kye sent a rider to Jubilee, for the doctor. Not that Granny Tate woman. Kye didn't want a darkie touching his father. Didn't seem right. Granny Tate had been on hand when Kye's sister Eugenia had her baby a couple of years back, but now Jubilee was a full-blown town, and there was a doctor there. The doctor wasn't much older than Kye, but he had been trained in school back east. Doctor Martin, he was called, young and skinny and in a three-piece suit, and he came out to the ranch and determined Tom Willbury had fractured his skull in the fall.

"I think there's bleeding inside his cranium," the doctor had said.

Kye didn't know quite what Doc Martin meant by the word *cranium*, but by the way Doc had said it, Kye figured bleeding in there couldn't be good.

Kye said, "Is there anything you can do?"

The doctor shook his head and looked a little sad. "Maybe someday, with the advances they're making in medicine. But not today, or any time soon."

"How long does he have?"

The doctor shrugged his shoulders. "He might not last the night. Or if the bleeding should stop, he might last days. He might even gain consciousness. I don't mean to give you false hope. It's just that with the human brain, we really don't know. It's the most important organ, but we know so little about it. I would say hope for the best," and the doctor gave Kye a solemn look, "but expect the worse."

His father hadn't died. But Kye couldn't call this being alive, either.

Eugenia and her husband had been living in a

small cabin out behind the main house, but once Pa had taken ill, they moved into the main house to help Kye with things.

Kye was in a vest and a range shirt. He wore jeans and riding boots. His father had taken to wearing a white shirt and a string tie during the day, as befitting the owner of one of the largest ranches in the area. But Kye felt out of place in a tie.

Kye considered himself a cowhand, and he dressed as such. His dad was the leader, the man everyone rallied behind. Kye really wanted nothing more than to be on the back of a horse, doing the work of a cowhand.

But here he was, attempting to run the ranch in what amounted to his father's absence. Trying to make the hard decisions.

He heard hoofbeats outside. Sounded like three riders. He looked over to the roll top desk against one wall. The top was rolled up, and on the flat surface under the roll top were ledger books, and a bottle of ink and a pen. And his gunbelt. He buckled the gunbelt on and headed out to the front porch.

Three riders pulled up. Frank, Till and Jones. Cowhands for the ranch. On the horse behind Frank was Jimmy Leonard, and Leonard's younger brother Brisk was behind Till. Second-rate gunfighters Kye had met at the Second Chance a month ago and offered them a job.

Neither man had his boots on.

Kye said, "What's going on?"

Jimmy Leonard jumped down from the back of Frank Lasky's horse and stood in the dirt in his socks.

"Mister Willbury, sir, we got bushwhacked."

Brisk jumped down, too. "I wouldn't say we got bushwhacked, exactly."

Jimmy said, "Shut yer mouth, Brisk."

Kye said, "Tell me what happened."

"Well..,"

Kye said, "I paid you to do a job. Tell me what

happened."

"It was one of the McCabe men, sir. He rode up to the dry streambed. We took a couple of shots at him. You know, to scare him off."

"Didn't work," Brisk said. "He got the drop on us and made us take our boots off and walk back."

Frank Lasky said, "We found 'em about eight miles back. Figured we'd ride 'em up to the main house."

Kye nodded. "You did right."

He looked at Jimmy Leonard. "Who done it? The old man himself?"

Leonard shrugged. "Don't rightly know. Didn't give his name."

Brisk said, "He had long, blonde hair. Had it tied back, like an Injun."

"Josh McCabe," Kye said. "You both are lucky to be alive."

"Yes, sir."

"You shot at him?"

They both nodded.

"How many times?"

Brisk said, "I fired three shots. Jimmy fired two."

Kye's hair was falling down into his eyes again. He reached up to brush it back. "And you didn't hit him?"

Brisk looked downward and shuffled his feet. "No, sir."

A woman came out the door. Thin and tired-looking, with hair as red as Kye's.

She said, "Kye? What's going on?"

He said, "Eugenia, go back inside. I'll handle this."

"Did you really tell these men to shoot at McCabe riders?"

Kye looked at Frank and the others. "You boys go grab some coffee. I'll come talk to you in a few minutes."

The boys nodded, and began turning away. Probably for the bunkhouse, Kye figured. There was usually coffee there. He remembered the days when he would have been with them. The days before his father had been injured.

He stepped back into the great room and Eugenia followed.

She had lips that looked a little swollen, and Kye thought her eyes looked like she had just got done crying. She had always looked that way, for as long as he could remember.

"Kye," she said. "What's going on?"

"I'm trying to run the ranch, is what's goin' on. I ain't Paw. I'll never claim to be. But I'm doin' what I can."

She put her hands on her hips. "But shootin' at McCabe cowhands? At Josh McCabe, himself?"

"I've gotta defend the range that's ours, Genie."

"What'll Paw say? When he's better?"

"He ain't getting' better, Genie!" Kye didn't mean to shout, but he found he couldn't hold it back. "He ain't said nary a word or opened his eyes in months. If he was gonna, he would have by now."

He stopped a moment, drew a breath, and reached one hand to the back of his neck to rub away the tension.

He said, more quietly, "It's up to me, now, to keep this place goin'."

Eugenia nodded her head, but said nothing.

"I ain't a leader, Genie. Not like Paw was. But I'm doin' my best."

"I know you are, Kye. So, what do we do now?"

"I've gotta go get your husband, and Frank and the boys. Josh McCabe's prob'ly on his way out here, and he ain't gonna be happy. Prob'ly have that outlaw brother of his with him and maybe even his father."

"Johnny McCabe hisself?"

"The boys and I have gotta be ready when they get here."

9

Josh and Dusty each had a Winchester carbine in one hand, and they reined up in front of the Willbury ranch house.

Kye Willbury stepped out, and he had an old Henry in his hands.

Newt Wood was with him. Newt had been ramrod for the ranch for the past few years, and he had married Eugenia a while back. Newt was twenty-five and had a narrow build and a narrow chin. He was in a brown shirt, and a vest that was a tattered old holdover from a three-piece suit. He wore a pistol on his hip, and he also had a rifle in his hands.

Kye said to Josh and Dusty, "That's far enough, boys. I don't want any trouble. You'd best turn around and ride back the way you came."

A man came into view over the peak of the roof, and he had a Winchester and it was aimed directly at Josh. Two more stepped around from the side of the house with rifles pressed to their shoulders and aimed at both Josh and Dusty.

Kye said, "We don't want trouble, but if you raise them rifles or go for your side arms, we'll shoot you both out of the saddle."

"You don't want trouble?" Josh roared. "It was your men who shot at me out on the range."

"Kye," Dusty said, his voice calm. "Where's your father? Maybe we should speak with him."

Kye said, "Any speakin' you have to do will be done with me. Now turn around and ride back the way you come."

Josh looked at Dusty, and Dusty raised one hand in a *slow down* motion.

Josh drew a breath and said, "Kye. I was out there today, at those rocks we call the Twin Sisters. Those two pieces of rock that shoot up beside each other."

"I know what rocks you mean," Kye said.

"They're clearly on McCabe range."

"I wasn't aware you'd filed claim on that section of range."

Dusty said, "That's all open range. But unofficially, we always claimed right up to the stream. We got one side, and you got the other."

"That's right," Kye said. "And that's the way it still is."

Josh said, "Then why'd you have men out there to shoot at me?"

"You was on our side of the stream."

Josh gave an acquiescing nod of the head, loaded with impatience. "Well, yeah. Where the stream is now. But not the old stream bed. That's the border."

Kye shook his head. "The border is the stream itself. My father and yours agreed to that a long time ago."

"The stream bed. Not the water itself."

"That ain't the way I understood it."

Josh felt the fury fading. He wasn't sure if he should be exasperated or laughing.

He said, "Kye, where's your father?"

"Where my father is ain't none of your business."

Josh looked at Dusty. Dusty shrugged his shoulders.

Josh said, "All right, Kye. I don't know what game you're playing, but I'm gonna let you off the hook. This time. But we're starting our spring roundup in a three of days. And we're gonna use whatever part of our range we need to. Do you understand what I'm saying, Kye? *Our* range."

"You show up on our side of the river, you'll get yourself shot."

Josh nodded. "You tell your father that if anyone shoots at us, this time we won't be sending men back without their boots. We'll be sending them back dead, draped over a horse."

Dusty said, "We don't want trouble, Kye. Your men fired the first shots. Let's bury this, now."

Kye said, "Get off this ranch, both of you. You're trespassin'."

Josh didn't really know what to think about any of this. He looked at Dusty and gave a sort of shrug with his brows. They turned their horses and started away down the trail.

As they rode away, Eugenia stepped out onto the porch.

She said, "Kye, are you out of your mind? Do you really think you can win a range war with them people? Because that's what this is gonna turn into if you don't stop it right now."

"A man has to make a stand."

Newt called out to the men. "Make sure they're gone, then you boys can all stand down."

Newt said to Kye, "I'll stay out here and watch over things. Make sure them McCabes don't come back."

Kye nodded and went inside. He tried to manage a strong stride as he crossed the floor to a horizontal gun rack mounted on a wall. A Winchester and a shotgun were there, and he returned his own rifle to its place among them.

The Winchester was a better rifle than the old Henry he used, but the Winchester was Paw's. The Henry was the old gun Paw had given to Kye when Paw got the Winchester. Kye hadn't wanted to use the Winchester. It seemed to Kye that to use his father's gun was to admit his father would never again be using it. Despite what he had said to Eugenia earlier, he wasn't ready to accept the reality that Paw would never again wake up.

Eugenia had followed him inside.

She said, "Kye, what's going on? That land out there, it don't belong to us, any more than it belongs to them. It's open range. We have an agreement with the McCabes. If one of them rides onto our side, we got no legal rights to kick 'em off. And even if we did, since when do we shoot at McCabes? Or them at us? We've all lived side-by-side here in these hills for a long time."

"I've made a decision, as the head of this ranch. We're gonna claim that section of range. Squatter's rights. We just gotta keep others off of it for seven years. I done talked to a lawyer about it, last summer. Down in Bozeman. He called it..," Kye hesitated, trying to remember the term, "inverse possession, or something like that. We gotta keep others off the acreage we're claiming, and we have to do it without no question."

She said, "You're still mad about Bree McCabe, ain't you?"

He looked away. "Don't know what you're talkin' about."

"Kye, that was five years ago."

"There weren't no reason she couldn't dance with me. None at all. But she was too good for me. That's what it was. She looked down her high-and-mighty McCabe nose at me. Then they announced she was getting' married, to that new-comer, from Texas or wherever he's from. Fat Cole. I mean, what kind of name is that?"

"I thought his name was Charles."

"Don't matter what his name is."

She put her hands on her hips. "Thomas Hezekiah Willbury. You're mad because she married someone else."

"No I ain't. I don't care what she does. She wants to marry that tall, skinny Texan, it's her business. But none of 'em are gonna set foot on land that we're claimin'."

She looked at him with disbelief.

He said, "We're family. We're supposed to stand together."

"Oh, I'm standin' with you, Kye. I just hope it don't get us all killed."

10

Haley sat on a swing, out on the front porch of the little cabin she and Dusty shared. Jonathan was on the swing with her, and they had a book. A first grade reader. Though Jonathan was not quite three, Haley believed it was good to read to a child.

She heard hoofbeats from somewhere down the trail. Someone was riding up, keeping the horse to a trot.

It was Bree, Haley knew, before she even saw her. When Bree was on Midnight, the horse often moved along at a pace that Haley called a *happy trot*. Bree had a way of often looking happy to simply be alive, and Midnight seemed to feel it when they were riding along.

Bree came into view and reined up at the porch.

"Aunt Bree," Jonathan said, and he ran down from the porch.

Bree scooped him up in a hug.

"So what brings you out here this morning?" Haley said.

"Oh, I just wanted to say hello, and invite you and Jonathan to join us for lunch. Cora wants to play cowboys and Indians."

Jonathan's eyes lit up. "Can I, Ma?"

Haley smiled. "I don't see why not. But I do have to be back in time to cook supper for Daddy."

"Aunt Temperence will cook enough for all of us!"

Haley and Bree were laughing.

Bree said, "That she will."

Bree was in a gray split skirt and a matching jacket. She wore black riding boots, and her hair was tied in a braid that fell down her back.

Haley said, "How about a cup of tea, first. Want to join me?"

Bree said, "Sure."

Haley went into the kitchen to put on a kettle of water, and Bree followed her. Haley sat Jonathan at the kitchen table with his book.

Bree said, "I do worry about you and Dusty a little. You're not that far from the main house, but you seem so isolated."

"I kind of like it," Haley said. "It's like our own little hideaway."

"Ma!" Jonathan called out.

But they heard it too. A wagon bouncing along the trail, behind a team of horses that was being pushed to almost a full gallop.

Haley and Bree went running to the front porch with Jonathan behind them. Henry Freeman was on the seat of a buckboard, pulling the reins to bring the team to a halt by the porch.

"Miss Haley," he said. His eyes were wide with what Haley thought was fear. "It's Granny Tate. You gotta come. I think she's dyin'."

Haley looked at Bree.

Bree said, "Go. I'll take Jonathan to the main house."

Without another thought about tea, Haley grabbed a pair of saddle bags from the house—Dusty had gotten them for her, to keep her doctoring supplies. She climbed into the wagon, and without another word, Henry turned the team around and they started down the trail.

11

Granny Tate was in bed. She looked so thin, much more so than the last time Haley had seen her, which was just the day before. Granny's eyes were sunken in and her cheeks hollow.

Haley took a chair beside the bed. Henry had walked in behind her, and he said, "Granny, Haley's here to see you."

At first, Granny Tate didn't react, but then her eyes fluttered open.

She looked at Haley, and allowed herself a weary smile. "Oh, child. It's good to see you."

"What can I do?" Haley said.

Granny shook her head. "Nothin', child. I'm dyin'. That's all."

"Dying?" Haley almost jumped out of her chair. "But Granny, you can't die."

"We *all* die, child. Now it's my turn, that's all."

"But what'll we do? I can't imagine you not being here. We need you."

Granny Tate shook her head. "Everyone has you, now. You'll be the granny woman."

"But there's so much I don't know. I've only been training with you for a year and a half."

Granny said, "You'll do fine, child. Trust yourself."

Haley nodded. But she wasn't so sure.

Granny looked over at Henry. She said, "Henry, fetch me my book."

He nodded. He reached under her bed and pulled out a volume. It had a tattered leather cover, and the binding was crumbling.

Granny Tate said, "I suppose there's no more reason to keep it hidden. Just old habits die hard, I suppose."

Henry handed it to Haley.

Granny said, "Open it up, child."

Haley opened the cover. There were pages of notes. Recipes, not for meals, but for tinctures and teas for healing. Some pages were loose, and others attached to the binding. Some pages were yellow and brittle-feeling, and others felt like newer paper. There were penciled drawings of various herbs and roots.

"That's all I know," Granny Tate said. "Everything I ever learned about doctorin'. How to set a broken bone is in there. How to remove a bullet." She chuckled. "I added that part after I met Johnny. Even at my age, I was still learnin'."

Haley couldn't help but grin.

"As a granny woman, you never stop learning. Every day, you learn something new. Your training never stops, even after your teacher is gone. The very job itself becomes your teacher."

Haley said, "I didn't know you were making such a book."

Granny nodded. "I began it back in the old days, when I first began studying with a granny doctor. Back when I was younger'n you. Back then, you see I was a slave. It was long before the War. And back then, it was against the law for a slave to learn to read or write."

Granny was looking off toward the ceiling, but she wasn't seeing the ceiling. She was seeing a time from long ago.

*   *   *

Tate Farm, Virginia
1796

Helen was fourteen years old, and she was running through the woods. She was in a linsey-woolsey dress that fell to her calves, and her feet were bare. The sticks underfoot stung a little as she ran, and at one point she stepped on an acorn and it hurt so bad she almost used a word her mama would not have wanted her to say.

But Helen didn't let the pain stop her. She had to

move. Massa Tate had been hurt, and Helen had been sent to find the granny woman.

Massa Tate wasn't a bad massa. Not like some that Helen had heard of. He treated his people with decency. Gave them cabins to live in that had wooden floors, and the boards of the walls were tight to keep out the cold of the winter. She had heard of some of the horrible things that happened to slaves at other places. Whippings and such. Massa Tate wouldn't let a whip be taken to his people.

It wasn't a huge plantation. More of a big farm. It was only Helen, her parents and her three brothers who worked there. Often Massa Tate worked alongside Helen's father and brothers.

That was how Massa Tate got hurt. He was in a buckboard riding beside the fence, talking to Helen's father. For some reason, the horse bolted, making the wagon lurch, and Massa Tate fell hard onto the fence. The rail was old and partly rotted, and it broke and the jagged end was driven into his ribs. Driven deep. Mrs. Tate said they should send for a doctor.

"I don't want no danged city doctor from up north touchin' me," he said. "That boy in town is from Philadelphia. I wouldn't let him touch me if I was dyin'."

There was a granny woman who lived in a cabin in the woods, out beyond the farm. Mrs. Tate sent Helen to fetch her.

Helen found her kneeling in a small garden outside the cabin. The cabin was made of logs, and in the garden were all sorts of plants that Helen knew nothing of. Helen had been here before, and the granny woman called it her *herb garden*.

The granny woman had long white hair and pale skin, and her face was taking on some lines.

"Granny!" Helen called out. "Come quick! It's Massa Tate!"

The Granny Woman often rode a mule bare-back, and that's how she came to the Tate Farm. Helen was on the mule behind her.

Massa Tate had been moved to the main house and was in his bed. Mrs. Tate had tied up a wad of sheet around the wound to stop the bleeding.

He was growing warm. Granny removed the sheet to check out the wound and prodded around a bit.

She said, "There's still a piece of wood inside him. It must have broken off. It has to come out."

Granny had young Helen assist her. Helen found she wasn't afraid or appalled by all of the blood. As Granny cut into the wound to find the sliver of wood, Helen found herself fascinated by the inner-workings of the body.

Granny pulled out piece of wood that was four inches long and half an inch wide. "Look at it," Granny said. "It's rotten. The infection from this would have killed him. As it is, it tore into stomach muscles. He's going to be a while healing."

Granny fixed Massa Tate some kind of tea to help him sleep, and she prepared a second kind with a touch of silver for infection.

"He should be all right," Granny said.

Mrs. Tate was a matronly woman, with a white linen cap that fit about her head like a bonnet, and an apron tied about her middle. Helen didn't think she had ever seen Mrs. Tate without an apron.

Mrs. Tate fixed some tea for herself and Granny, and they sat at the kitchen table.

Mrs. Tate said, "What would we ever do without you?"

"That's a good question. A granny woman can't live forever, and I'm pushing sixty now."

Helen was still there. She said, "I'd love to be a granny woman."

Mrs. Tate gave the child a warm smile, the way you give a child who has said something endearing but a little silly.

"I've never heard of a colored girl being a granny woman."

Granny shrugged her shoulders. "I don't see why not. She was very helpful with Mister Tate, and she has always been a curious child. When she visits my cabin, she always asks questions, and they're the right questions. You can tell a lot about a child's intelligence and inclinations by the questions they ask. If you and her mother give me permission, I can begin teaching her."

Mrs. Tate gave the notion a thoughtful nod of her head. "I'll talk with Mister Tate about it."

When Granny visited the next day to check on her patient, she found him awake and sitting up in bed. He fully approved of the idea of Granny teaching Helen.

"There's one problem," Granny said. "To do this properly, I'll have to teach her to read."

Tate gave a knowing nod of his head. "That could get us all in a whole boat-load of trouble."

"And yet, if she's going to be taught, she has to be taught right."

Tate gave it a little thought. "All right. But it has to be done at your cabin, and it has to be done in secret. No one can be allowed to know that Helen is going to know how to read."

On Helen's first day of formal training, she said, "How come they call you Granny? I never see any grandchildren around."

Granny smiled. "I never married, dear."

"Then, why do they call you Granny?"

"That's a title that comes with the job of being a granny woman or a granny doctor. They were calling me granny when I was eighteen. My real name is Clarice."

"So," Helen was a little amused at the thought, "they're gonna call me Granny someday, even if I'm not a grandmother."

"That they will. And I have the feeling you're going to be a fine granny woman."

*   *

*

Clarice died when Helen was nineteen years old. She was buried on the Tate farm, in the small cemetery out back. The cemetery where Massa Tate's parents were buried.

"She was my niece, you know," Tate said. "Daughter of my brother."

Helen nodded. "She mentioned that, Massa."

"I guess you're the granny woman now."

Helen had been so crushed at the death of the woman who was her mentor, that the full weight of the new reality hadn't really settled on her. She was now the area's granny woman.

Tate said, "You should have the cabin, for your own. It's on my land, actually. And I'm going to give you your freedom papers, so you can come and go as you like without anyone hassling you."

Helen nodded. Freedom. She had never been free in her life. When she was younger, she used to wonder what it felt like. But over the past few years, she had been so busy training with Granny and assisting her with birthings and those who were ill, with setting bones and such, that she hadn't given it much thought. Granny even assisted with sick animals, and delivered more than one colt.

*   *

*

Tate Farm
1865

The farm house had collapsed, and the remains were charred and smoldering. Yankee soldiers had burned the house and driven off the slaves.

Part of their war effort was to liberate the slaves, but every so often they found slaves who refused to

48

leave. That was what happened on the Tate farm. This place was home to Helen's family, the only home they had ever known. So the soldiers drove them off.

It had been the same with the home of Robert E. Lee. Not that Helen had been there, but she had heard about it afterward. Lee had freed his slaves some time before, but they had remained voluntarily on the plantation. When the northern soldiers came, they drove the former slaves off.

Helen was now 83, and had been called Granny most of her life. Her hair had now turned white, and her knees were a little rickety, especially in the morning. She was thinking of cutting herself a stick to use as a cane.

She had never married. A granny woman was often too busy to have a family. In more civilized parts, where there were school-trained doctors, it would have been different. But here in the Alleghenies, a granny woman was all they had, and they kept her busy.

Old Massa Tate and his wife were in the cemetery out back. Granny had tended to them as they were dying. She had brought their grandson Terrence into the world, and he had become owner of the farm. The soldiers had killed him when they burned the house.

Granny stood in front of the house, staring at the loss.

Henry Tate came walking up to her. He had been driven away, but once the soldiers left, he came back.

He was a young black man, firmly muscled and with a square jaw. A smile that made you want to smile along with him. But there wasn't much to smile about, these days.

He was actually the grandson of her brother. She had brought Henry into the world, too. People assumed she was his grandmother, and she didn't mind the thought so never corrected them. Neither did he.

He said, "It's all gone, Granny. Our home. Everything we knew."

She nodded. "My cabin, too. The cabin of the

granny doctor who trained me. The only home I've had for sixty-three years. I managed to save my book, though."

"We're leavin', Granny. Livvy and me. We're taking the children and we're going."

She looked at him? "Going? Where are you gonna go?"

"West. There's a wagon that wasn't destroyed by the Yankees, and we have horses. Come with us, Granny."

"But I've lived in these hills all my life. I don't know if I could live anywhere else. These hills, and the people in these hills, are all I know."

"Most of the people you know are gone now. Life around here ain't never gonna be the same."

Granny gave a long sigh. She didn't really want to leave, but there was no reason to stay.

"All right."

Then he said, "I'm changing my name. There ain't no slavery, anymore. I'm a free man. So that's what I'm gonna call myself. Henry Freeman."

"The Tates was good people, Henry. They treated us well."

He nodded. "That they did. They treated us with more kindness than any other massas I've ever heard of. But it's still not the same as bein' free."

She gave him a long look. "No, it's not."

*   *

*

McCabe Ranch, Montana
1868

Granny Tate sat in a fine chair, facing a huge, stone hearth. In one hand was a cup and saucer, and sitting before her in a rocker was one of the finest white ladies she had ever met. Like something out of one of the grandest plantations of the old South. Not someone

Granny would have expected to meet in remote Montana Territory. The woman's name was Ginny.

Sitting in a chair of pine wood and cowhide was Johnny McCabe. He was in his mid-thirties, with his hair long and tied back, like Granny had seen with some Indians. He wore two guns, and he rode a horse like he and the horse were one.

They had invited her and the Freemans to visit, as a way of welcoming them to the area.

"I must admit," the grand white lady said, "I have never heard the term *granny woman*, before."

Granny explained what it meant, and what a granny woman's duties were.

"I heard the term when I was growing up in Pennsylvania," Johnny said. "My grandfather often told stories of when he was young and that area was still frontier. He spoke of a granny woman."

Henry was there, sitting on the sofa with Livvy. Henry had a cup of strong coffee, and Livvy was drinking tea.

Henry had been uneasy with the whole idea of accepting an invitation from these people, especially in their home.

Henry said, "I have to say, Mister McCabe, I find this a little odd. It ain't every day you see a white man inviting a black man into his home."

"Henry," Granny said.

"No, that's all right," Johnny said. "It's true. You don't see it every day. But maybe the world would be a better place if you did."

Henry nodded. "You got a point."

*   *
*

As Haley looked at the book, Granny said, "Johnny McCabe is unlike any man I have ever met. He not only says things like, *you should do the right thing just because it's the right thing to do*, he actually does it.

Henry has said Johnny is the first white man he ever trusted. And Johnny never violated the trust."

Haley nodded. "He's raised his sons that way, too. It's the way Dusty and I are raising Jonathan."

Henry had stepped out, and it was just Haley and Granny in the room. Student and teacher.

Granny Tate said, "In the early days, being a granny woman meant you had no time for a family. The people living in the hills around you—they was your family. But even though you're a wife and a mother, I think you'll do fine. Folks today, they's more civilized. They go to the school-trained doctor in town. But you'll still have people knockin' at your door, needin' your help."

"Granny, I don't want to lose you."

Granny smiled. "You won't lose me, child. The body might die away, as each does in its own time, but the spirit lives on."

Haley nodded. A tear was rolling down her face. "Pa says things like that, too."

"One of the reasons I like him so much."

Granny went to sleep, and Haley thought, after hearing Granny's story, maybe tea sounded like a good idea. She set the book down on the chair and went out to the kitchen.

Livvy had a blue bandana tied down over her hair like a bonnet, and she was at the stove with water heating.

She said, "I figured you'd want tea. Never knew a granny woman who didn't like her tea."

When the tea was ready, Livvy and Haley sat at the table. Livvy talked about how they had settled in Texas first, then made their way to Montana. How she and Henry had a son who was still in Texas, working as a drover.

"I don't know if I can do this," Haley said. "Be a granny woman. Maybe if I had more years of training. Granny trained with her teacher for five full years."

Livvy reached over and took Haley's hand. "You'll

do fine. There's a certain way about a granny woman. I've met more than one. They have a certain look in the eye. A certain energy about them. You have that same way. Granny said to me a few weeks ago that you were born to be a granny woman. I think she's right."

Haley went back into the bedroom to check on Granny, and she found Granny had passed. There was a smile on Granny's face, and her eyes were shut as though she was sleeping.

"Granny," Haley said, "be well and be safe. I'll take care of everyone. Just like you taught me."

12

Josh and Jack bellied up to the bar at the Second Chance. The barroom was empty at the moment, except for Hunter. He was sitting on a stool behind the counter with a newspaper open.

Josh said, "Been a slow day?"

Hunter shrugged. "It's a Wednesday. The afternoon stage is due in a little while. We'll get a little business, then. Let me guess, cold beers for you two?"

"I can go down and get them," Josh said.

"Naw, that's all right. Gives me somethin' to do."

He laid the paper across the bar and headed off to the root cellar.

Jack said, "I guess I never really knew much about the Willburys. I see Tom and his son Kye in here from time to time. Though I don't think I've seen Tom for a while."

"They stay to themselves, mostly," Aunt Ginny said, walking in through the open doorway to the restaurant side of the establishment. "I thought I heard voices in here. I hope you two weren't going to have a drink without saying hello."

"Wouldn't think of it," Josh said. "But we didn't want to bother you if you were busy."

"Not at all. We'll have some business once the stage pulls in. And tonight the dining room will be full. This is what I suppose could be called the afternoon lull."

Josh told her about his run-in with the Willburys. While he was talking, Hunter returned with two mugs of cold beer.

She said, "There has never been trouble with the Willburys, before."

Hunter shook his head. "Old Tom Willbury hardly ever even comes to town. I don't know when I last saw him. Been a while, I guess."

"They have always seemed somewhat reclusive. But then, their ranch is farther away from town than ours."

Josh said, "About fifteen miles. But it's not an easy fifteen miles. Lots of hills. And the road becomes impassible in the winter."

Josh heard footsteps at the barroom door and glanced over. It was Eugenia Willbury. She was in a hat and shawl. He hadn't seen her in months, maybe longer, but she looked about the same as she always had. Thin and awkward, and with a face that was pale and freckled. Her eyes looked like she had just been crying. She was married now, but Josh didn't remember her married name.

"Speak of the devil," Josh said. "Sort of."

"Josh McCabe," she said, as she came up to the bar. "And Jack. I was here to see Miss Ginny. But it's so fortuitous that you're here. You're really the ones I need to talk to."

She spoke a little stiffly, like she was using words she wasn't used to. Maybe trying a little too hard to seem erudite, the way some folks do when they feel inferior to the people they're talking to.

Then she looked at Ginny and gave a quick, partial curtsey. "Miss Ginny."

Ginny nodded. "Eugenia."

"I'm in town for supplies," Eugenia said. "Mister

Franklin's loadin' my wagon, but I got a little time. Can we get a table and talk? All of us? I think my brother's plumb out of his mind, and he's gonna get someone shot."

They took a table, and Eugenia talked. About her father, and about Kye.

Ginny said, "I'm so sorry to hear about your father, Eugenia. I had no idea."

"Most folks don't. It was Kye's idea to keep it a secret. He said family business is private business."

"We're all neighbors. We need to be there for each other."

"That's how I feel. But Kye—he has this idea that we have to take care of ourselves. Pa was like that, too. Like when the barn burned three years ago. He and Kye and the men cut logs and hauled them in from the ridges. They split them into boards and rebuilt the barn themselves. Wouldn't take no help from no one."

Josh said, "I hadn't heard your barn burned."

"That's what I mean. Anyone else, there would have been a barn raisin'. Neighbors from all over. Could have had that new barn built in a day. But not Pa. And Kye's just like him."

She and Ginny each had a cup of tea in front of them. Josh and Jack were sipping their beer.

Ginny said, "Why does your brother want to keep riders off your family's section of open range?"

"He's trying to claim everything north of the stream for the ranch. He's says he talked about squatter's rights with a lawyer down in Bozeman. He says it's something called inverse action."

Jack said, "Adverse possession."

Josh looked at Jack. "Does he have any legal grounds?"

Jack shrugged. "Possibly. But to do so he has to keep everyone off of the range for so many years. Seven, I believe is the accepted length of time in Montana Territory at the moment. I would have to look it up."

"But," he looked at Eugenia, "your father and ours

agreed on the old stream's location as the unofficial dividing line."

She shrugged. "Kye's not listening to reason."

Ginny said, "I have the feeling there is more going here than just grazing rights."

Eugenia nodded. "He's still mad. Remember when he asked Bree to a dance years ago, and she said no?"

Josh didn't remember. He looked at Jack.

Jack said, "I was home that summer, from school. Wasn't it five years ago?"

Eugenia nodded. "He ain't forgotten. And he asked Bree to a picnic after that, one Sunday after church, and she said no. Then when he heard she was marrying that cowhand of yours from Texas, he got mad all over again."

Jack said, "Isn't that kind of obsessive on his part?"

She said, "It's crazy, is what it is. But Kye's always been a little different."

Josh brought his beer up for a sip, primarily to stifle a grin. He wanted to say that *different* is sure a word for Kye. Josh had always thought Kye was awkward and backward, to the point of being comical.

She said, "But he is my brother. That's why I'm here. I don't want anyone hurt. Do you have to go near that stream? Can't you just let Kye have it?"

Josh took a sip of beer. "It's not the acreage. It's that the stream is the only usable water in that area. We might have to use it during roundup. I rode out to check the area, and most of the streams that fill up during spring runoff are already running dry. After that blizzard we had just before Christmas, we didn't get much more snow. Runoff is light, this year."

"All I ask is that you consider it," she said. "He's my brother. I don't want any harm to come to you or yours, but I don't want any to come to him, either."

Josh said, "I'll do what I can. But I have to be honest. Grazing rights and water rights are the life blood of a ranch. I don't want to take anything that's not ours, but I'm not going to let anything be taken away from us."

She nodded. "I understand."

Ginny said to her, "Would it help any if I went out and talked with Kye?"

"No, ma'am, I don't think so, but thanks for offering." Eugenia got to her feet, and Josh and Jack did, too.

She said, "I'd best be heading back."

Josh said, "One thing I can guarantee. If there is a first shot fired, it won't be from us. That I can promise."

"Thank you, Josh. I guess that's all I can ask."

Jack and Josh waited until she had stepped back out onto the street, then they sat back down.

Jack said, "I'll research property rights. See what I can find out."

Josh nodded.

Aunt Ginny said, "I had no idea Tom Willbury was in that kind of condition."

"None of this would be happening if old Tom was still running the place," Josh said. "His boy Kye was never right in the head."

"This could get bad, couldn't it?"

Josh nodded. "Yes'm, I'm afraid it could."

13

Eugenia went in to check on her father. He was lying on his back, his eyes shut, breathing easily. Just like every single day since he had been thrown by his horse.

She reached down to touch his forehead. He didn't seem any warmer than he should be. The doctor had said sometimes fever can hit someone who's in a coma. Something like a cold can turn into pneumonia real easy. But Paw seemed all right.

She turned and left the room.

The house was all on one floor, essentially a long log cabin. The floors were a little uneven in places, but Eugenia knew there were many sod huts and log cabins that had dirt floors. Her Paw had worked hard to provide the best for her and Kye.

She stepped out into the parlor. Kye was there, and so was Newt. They each had a drink in their hands. A glass of something brown. She didn't know what it was, but she knew it was liquor.

"Kye," she said. "Newt. You know Paw don't allow liquor on the ranch."

"Well, I'm in charge now," Kye said, "and I make the rules."

She stared at him with disbelief. "Paw ain't dead, Kye. He's just down the hall. And he just might get better. What then?"

"Well, then he'll be running things again. But until then, I'm in charge."

Newt said, "Be easy on him, Genie. We're just havin' a drink for luck."

"What do you need luck for?" she didn't like the sound of this.

Kye sat at the edge of Paw's desk. He said, "Well, I made me a decision. That's what."

"What kind of decision did you make?"

Newt looked at Kye, and Kye looked at him.

Eugenia said, "Someone better tell me what's goin' on."

Newt said, "You wanna tell her, or do I?"

Kye looked like he was trying to work up his courage. Like he knew she wasn't going to like what he was about to say.

He said, "I've gotta do what's best for this ranch, Genie. Sometimes Paw had to make decisions that were hard. Like, remember them rustlers, a couple of years ago?"

She nodded. "Paw hanged 'em."

"*We* hanged 'em. Paw was in charge, but Newt and me, we were right there with him. And Frank and Harmon. We done it. It was a hard decision, but it had to be done. There ain't no law out here, and we gotta take care of things ourselves."

She waited for more, but he wasn't offering more.

She said, "What decision have you made, Kye?"

He drew a breath and braced himself. "We're ridin' out to the McCabe ranch tonight. We're gonna pay them boys a visit and let 'em know what's what."

"You're riding out to the McCabe ranch? For what?"

"Like I said, we're gonna make it clear to 'em about that land out there. It belongs to this ranch."

She didn't like the look in their eyes. Part of it, she was sure, was the liquor. Whiskey, or whatever it was.

"Kye, you gotta promise me there won't be no trouble. This kind of thing can lead to a range war. People can get hurt. And them McCabes are gunfighters. Neither one of you is a gunfighter. You're cowhands."

Kye sprang off the edge of the desk and took a couple of quick steps toward her, his dander up. "You don't think I can stand up to your old boyfriend, Josh McCabe?"

"He ain't my boyfriend, Kye. Never was."

Newt said, "I remember years ago, when you was sweet on him. I thought you had let all of that go."

"Newt," she said. "I ain't sweet on Josh McCabe. All right, maybe I was once. But that was a long time ago."

She looked at Kye. "But they're gunfighters, Kye. Josh and Dusty, and their father. The men who work for them are, too."

Kye said, "And you don't think dumb old, backwards cowhands like us can stand up to them, huh?"

"Just promise me you won't start no trouble. I don't want anyone hurt. Specially you two."

Newt grinned, and reached up to the side of her face. "Don't worry about us, sweetie. We can take care of ourselves."

"Just see that you do. No little chunk of land is worth anyone getting shot over."

Kye downed the rest of his liquor and set the glass on the desk. "Come on, let's go to the bunkhouse. I want Frank, Harmon and Jusky to ride along with us."

Newt nodded. He finished off his drink in one gulp, and the two headed outside.

This is bad, Eugenia thought. She knew her brother. He had always felt small around Josh McCabe, even though Kye was a couple of inches taller. And somehow he had never got over being stung by Bree.

She went back down the hall to Paw's room.

She pulled a chair beside the bed and sat.

"Paw," she said. "I don't know if'n you can hear me or not. I like to think you can. We got us a real problem. It's Kye. He's trying to run this ranch. He's trying to be the man you are. But I think he's trying too hard. I'm afraid his pride and his foolishness is going to lead him to starting a range war with the McCabes. And I just don't think that's a war he can win."

She drew a long breath. Her eyes were toward the far side of the room, but she wasn't looking at anything in particular.

"There was a time I was so in love with Josh McCabe, Paw. I never said anything, but I always figured you knew. I never had a woman around here to talk with, 'cause Maw died when I was so young, so I kept it to myself. But I used to be so in love. I wondered what it would be like to be his wife. To be raising a family with him. I always wondered if we would live at their ranch, or if he and I would live here.

"He and Kye would run the ranch with you, be you're right-hand men. The two family ranches could merge, and it would be the biggest danged ranch in the territory. And I would call Miss Brackston Aunt Ginny, like they do."

She giggled. "I got a confession, Paw. I always thought it kind of too bad you never remarried, and I used to wonder what it would be like if you married Miss Brackston. I mean, you are both about the same age. You was older when you first met Maw. You was near forty, and Maw was just a young thing, no older'n me."

She shook her head. "I let go of my McCabe fantasies long ago. Newt was here working at the ranch, and I had caught his fancy. I figured he was a good man, and now we got us a baby. A grandchild for you. Kye allowed me to use some ranch money to hire us a nanny, a darkie woman from in town. She helps take care of little Rebecca.

"Remember, she was named after Maw. She's walking, now. You'd be so proud of her."

She felt so weary. She leaned back in the chair, and reached up with both hands to rub the tension from her face.

"I'm afraid Kye and Newt are gonna go in there tonight and get themselves killed, Paw. The obvious answer to the problem with the land is to let both sides use it equal, but Kye don't see it that way. I don't think he wants to. I think he's still sore at Bree McCabe, and there ain't no reason for it. And I think he's always felt small around Josh. It's clouding his judgement."

She took a look at her father. "It would be so good if you could wake up, Paw. Take charge again. You're the only one Kye would ever listen to. I don't mean to rush you, and I know you would if you could. But we need you, Paw."

She realized she wasn't sure if Paw was breathing. When she checked on him earlier, he had been breathing slowly and gently, like he was just asleep. But now he seemed so still.

"Paw?" she said.

She got out of the chair and reached a hand to his mouth and nose, to see if there was any exhaling.

There seemed to be none.

"Paw?"

She took his wrist and felt for a pulse. There seemed to be none. She placed her ear against his chest. There was no heartbeat, and no breathing.

"Oh, Paw."

She sat back in the chair and looked at her father, and tears began streaming down her cheeks.

14

"We should send for the doctor," Eugenia said. "He might want to fill out a death certificate, or something. And we should send for the minister. That new one at the Methodist church, now that Tom McCabe is the town marshal."

Kye reared up, like he was standing as tall as he possibly could. He looked a little ridiculous, she thought, as skinny as he was and as baggy as his clothes looked on him, and with his orange hair falling past his brow into his eyes. He shook his head and the hair flew away, only to fall back over his brow.

He said, "We don't need no doctor or minister. We always took care of things ourselves on this ranch, and it ain't about to change now."

So, the very afternoon Tom Willbury had died, they buried him out behind the ranch house, beside their mother.

Eugenia stood looking down at the grave, feeling numb all over. Shock, disbelief. It didn't feel real to her that this man who had been the center of the family and the ranch could now just be gone, like he had never been here at all.

Kye was there, across the grave from her. Newt was at her side. She saw they were both wearing guns. There was no need for them to be wearing guns for a burial. It wasn't like they were McCabes, who seemed to wear their guns everywhere.

Then it occurred to her why they were armed.

She said, "Newt. Kye. You can't go through with your plan. All you'll do is provoke them people. You don't want to do that."

"I made a decision for the good of this ranch and this family," Kye said. "They decided to challenge me on it. It's on them, not me. We have to send them a message that we ain't to be messed with."

"Kye, they aren't messing with anyone. They just want to abide by the same agreement their Paw made with ours."

Newt said, "I was just talkin' to Heck, who got back from town a little while ago. He says their old man is out of town. Off on some cattle-buyin' trip, or something. So we won't have him to deal with."

"It don't matter," she said. "Dusty is still there, and Josh. That man Bree married--he's a gunfighter, too. Just look at him, the way he carries that gun. And that tall farmer in the valley—he ain't really no farmer. Have you seen the look in that man's eyes? You'll be fightin' all of them."

"They made the choice," Kye said.

"No, dang it. *You* made the choice. You're makin' it right now. Don't you see? Newt?" she looked at her husband. "Don't you see? They've gotta protect their grazing rights. Josh said so himself. Miss Ginny offered to come out and talk to you. Maybe I should'a taken her up on it."

"Miss Ginny?" Kye said. "Josh? When you been talkin' to them?"

She had said too much, she realized. They didn't know she had talked to Miss Ginny, Josh and Jack, when she had gone into town for supplies the day before.

"So," Newt said. "You been talkin' to Josh McCabe behind my back?"

"No, Newt. I just talked to 'em all when I went in town for supplies. I thought maybe if I talked to 'em, I could make sense of all this. But Josh is right. He has to protect his grazin' rights."

"The stream has always been the border between our range and theirs. It changed its course over the winter."

Newt said, "Good enough for me."

"Well," Eugenia said, "it's not for me."

"It don't matter," Kye said. "Paw's gone, now. I'm runnin' this ranch from now on, and Newt's my right-hand-man."

He glanced toward the sun. It was getting low in the sky.

Kye said, "Let's saddle up. I want to be just outside the pass that leads into the valley by sunset."

Newt nodded. "I'll go get the horses."

He gave Eugenia one long last look, and walked off toward the stables.

"Kye," she said. "You're just gonna get someone killed. Maybe yourselves."

"You never questioned Paw's decisions," he said. "I don't want you questioning mine. I've got a ranch to run, and if you don't want to stand behind me, then as far as I'm concerned, you can pack your things and leave."

He turned and walked away.

She said, though she knew he couldn't hear her, "I always stood behind Paw because he was right in the head. The same can't be said for you."

15

Josh had a glass of scotch in one hand and was standing by the hearth, leaning against the mantelpiece with one hand. His gunbelt was in his room upstairs.

Bree and Charles were on the sofa. They had been living in her room since their wedding, and they would be there until the cabin was ready.

Jessica was upstairs with the twins and Cora.

The only light in the room was from the fire, and firelight flickered against the walls. The windows were dark, and the quiet feeling of nighttime was in the air.

Temperence came downstairs. She said, "Jessica has gotten the twins down, and she's asleep herself.

Infants can wear you out. Cora's in bed too."

Temperence took the rocker by the hearth. Josh had poured a glass of wine for her, and it was standing on the mantel. He grabbed it and handed it to her.

She smiled a *thank you* at him.

Charles was sitting with his long legs stretched out in front of him. All that kept him from being the tallest man Josh had ever seen was Harlan Carter, who was even taller.

Charles said, "How concerned are you about the problem with the Willburys?"

Josh shrugged. "I don't really know what to think. They were always good neighbors. Stuck to themselves, for the most part. I saw Kye occasionally at Hunter's on a Saturday Night, but that was about all. And we'd see Eugenia in town getting supplies at Franklins."

Charles looked at Bree. "So, Kye had his eye on you, huh?"

It was Bree's turn to shrug. "I didn't think so. Yes, he asked me to dance, once. And he asked me to a church picnic. But there was never any feeling of anything between us. He was just the skinny, awkward son of Tom Willbury, with all that red hair."

She couldn't help but chuckle. "I never took him seriously. I didn't think he took himself seriously. I didn't know if he asked me because I was the only single girl within riding distance, or because his father put him up to it."

Temperence said, "Why would his father do that?"

"We were the only two ranches in the area for a long time. An alliance between the two ranches might make sense. Two good families, with two large ranches. Maybe Tom was looking at grandchildren. I don't know. I never thought much about it."

Josh said, "Maybe you should have taken him a little more seriously. Not laughed at him."

She gave him a look. "I didn't mean to laugh at him. It was just that he was standing there, too nervous to even look me in the eye. His hair was in a bowl cut back then, and it was growing out and it kept falling into his eyes. He kept trying to flip it back by shaking his head while he was talking to me, and all I could think of was a horse swishing his tail at flies."

Temperence was grinning. Charles was, too. He said to Bree, "Well, weren't you just the heartbreaker."

Bree said, "I was not."

Josh was laughing. "I remember how he was, back then. Not much different now."

"Well, you shouldn't talk, considering the crush Eugenia had on you."

This made him blink with surprise. "Me? When did she have a crush on me?"

Temperence looked at him with a big grin. "She had a crush on you?"

"No," he said. He looked at Bree. "She did not have a crush on me."

Bree said, "She most certainly did. Aunt Ginny and I used to laugh about it. We used to wonder what children between you two would look like."

Josh cringed. "She was all bony, with fat lips, and her eyes always looked like she had just gotten done bawling. And she would stand there and stare at me."

"That's because she had a crush on you."

"I thought it was just because she was a little tetched in the head, like her brother."

"Well," Bree broke into a big grin. "I didn't say she wasn't. Considering who she had the crush on."

"Hey."

Charles said, "So, have you decided about the roundup?"

"The best grass this spring seems to be north of the line cabin. But that puts us within distance of the stream. I don't want trouble with the Willburys, but we've got to do what's best for the ranch. I'm sending Ches out with the chuck wagon tomorrow morning, and Dusty's going to head out with the remuda. I'm going to send Kennedy and Taggart with them, and I was hoping maybe you could ride along, too."

"Absolutely, Boss."

"I don't expect any trouble, really. At least, I hope we don't have any."

Bree said, "I can't imagine Kye Willbury would have the gumption to actually carry through with his threats."

"I do wish Tom was up and about. He was always reasonable."

There was a shot from outside, and a window beside the front door shattered.

"Get down!" Josh shouted.

They all hit the floor.

Another shot was fired, and then a third. One bullet caught a stone on the hearth and zinged away.

Josh said to Temperence, "Stay down."

Then he and Charles crawled on hands and knees across the floor to the rifle rack. Josh pulled down a Winchester carbine and tossed it to Charles.

That was when Josh noticed Bree had crawled over, too.

"Bree," he said. "Get back there with Temperence."

She said, "Toss me my rifle."

He felt a wave of exasperation rush through him. This was his little sister, and he didn't want her getting hurt. But what was that term Pa was starting to use for her? Lady Gunhawk. Josh was trying to accept the notion that she was handier in a gun battle than most men he had known.

Two more shots were fired shattering another window, Josh pulled Bree's yellow boy from the rack and tossed it to her. He then grabbed a Winchester for himself.

These rifles were loaded. Pa had always said, keep your guns loaded and treat them like they're loaded. An empty gun does no one any good.

"I'll go upstairs," Bree said. "Make sure Jessica and the kids are all right, and I'll see if I can get a shot at them from one of the windows."

Before Josh could object or even comment, she got to her feet and said, "Cover me."

Josh went to a window, jacked a round into his rifle and began firing. Charles did the same. Not that they knew where the shots outside were being fired from, but maybe the return fire would send the men ducking for cover, and give Bree time to get across the room.

Bree covered the parlor floor at a run, and then charged up the stairs.

Josh called back to Temperence, "Are you all right?"

"I am. But, Josh. The kitchen door."

She was right, he realized. It was unguarded. Dang. Pa would have already thought about that. But Josh wasn't like Pa or Dusty. He was a cattleman and a horseman. He was learning not be ashamed of it, and to appreciate his own strengths. But he felt he should have thought about the kitchen door.

"I'll go," Charles said, and he began scampering on all fours across the floor toward the kitchen.

Josh crawled across the closed doorway to another window. He didn't want to remain in the same window he had fired from. His boots sent pieces of broken glass skittering away, and one piece of glass crunched under his knee. He felt one shard bite into his left hand.

He took a look at the darkness outside. In the moonlight, he could see the barn, standing dark and quiet. Stars were shining overhead.

Then there was a gunshot, and he saw the bright flash from the rifle. The bullet cut through the window frame where he had been.

He raised his rifle and fired a shot toward where the flash had been. Then he ducked, because he knew they would be able to see the flash from his own rifle.

Two shots came toward his window. One hit the wall outside the house, and the other went through the empty window frame.

"Temperence?" Josh called out.

"I'm all right. I'm flat on the floor, behind the sofa."

"Stay there."

"Oh, I'm not going anywhere."

He raised his rifle for another shot. There was a flash from beside the barn, another shot being fired at him. The bullet hit the window frame, and he ducked his head down.

He heard Bree's rifle bark from an upstairs window. Then he heard a shout from outside. Then there were more shots fired toward the house.

Shots were then fired from down by the bunkhouse. Old Ches was there, along with Kennedy and Taggart. They were probably returning fire.

Someone from out back shouted. Then another man shouted. He thought it was Charles' voice.

Then Charles came running back into the parlor. He said, "Taggart's got the kitchen door. Ches and Kennedy are further down. They think there's four shooters."

Josh said, "I think Bree may have gotten one, from upstairs."

There were more shots from out by the barn, and then more from Ches and Kennedy. Josh fired a shot. Charles went to a window and fired.

Then they waited. There were no more shots from the attackers.

Josh said to Charles, "I'm going outside. Cover me."

Charles nodded.

Josh reached up and opened the door, then went running outside onto the porch. He covered the porch steps in a leap, landed and rolled forward in a somersault, and came up on one knee, the rifle ready to fire.

There were no shots.

Kennedy came running over.

"Boss," he said. "Everyone all right in the house?"

Josh nodded. He rose to his feet. The knee he had injured years ago when Vic Falcone and his raiders had attacked the house was aching a little, after the leap and roll off the porch.

Kennedy said, "Looks like they're gone."

Ches came walking up. "I think they run off. They must have hid their horses out there in the dark, somewhere."

They heard the sound of iron-shod hooves on the wooden bridge, down by the river.

"Must be them," Ches said. "They must'a swum their horses across the river when they came in, or we would've heard 'em."

Kennedy looked at Josh. "Want us to saddle up and go after 'em?"

Josh shook his head. "We'd never catch 'em."

Then he had a thought.

"Come on," he said. "Bree might have hit one. Let's see."

They went around to the side of the barn, and in the moonlight, they found a man on the ground. A bullet hole was in his forehead.

"Ever seen him before?" Charles said.

Josh nodded. "He looks a lot like the jasper who was on the roof of the Willbury house, aiming a rifle at Dusty and me."

16

Josh sent Kennedy to fetch Dusty. While they were waiting, Josh saddled two horses himself.

A wagon came over the wooden bridge, the horse's hooves clattering, and then it came up the trail toward the house. Harlan Carter was at the reins, with his wife beside him.

He said, "Everything all right up here? We heard the gunfire from down at the house. We knew something was wrong."

His wife Emily had insisted on coming along, and she went inside to help. Glass shards were sprayed over most of the parlor floor, and a bullet had shattered a glass lamp Ginny had sent for from San Francisco, and coal oil had spilled everywhere.

Josh had buckled on his gunbelt and tucked a rifle into his saddle.

Carter said, "Looks like you're loaded for bear."

Josh nodded. "We know who did this. As soon as Dusty gets here, he and I are gonna take care of it."

Josh told Carter of the recent events.

Carter said, "Tom Willbury's son, hmm? Didn't think he had the backbone for something like that. Thought the Willburys had more honor, too."

"Old Tom does. But apparently he's not a factor in this."

"Want me to ride along?"

"Thanks, but no. I'd like you to stay here, if you don't mind. Bree's staying, and Charles and the men. I'd appreciate it if you'd help them keep the place safe."

Carter nodded. "I'll be here."

Another wagon was approaching, this one from the western edge of the valley. It was a buckboard, with Dusty holding the reins. Haley and Jonathan were beside him. Haley was in a nightgown and robe, and her hair was tied into a long braid. Kennedy was riding beside them.

Josh gave them a quick rundown.

"Is anyone hurt?" Haley said.

Josh shook his head. "We got lucky. But," he looked at Dusty, "you and I are gonna pay the Willburys a visit."

"Right now?" Haley said. "Shouldn't it wait till daylight?"

Dusty shook his head. "In a situation like this, you want the element of surprise on your side."

Dusty thought like Pa, and he had been raised by Sam Patterson. Josh felt better about his plan with Dusty agreeing to it.

Dusty's Spencer rifle was leaning against the wagon seat. He grabbed it and stuffed it into the saddle. Then he put his hands on Haley's shoulders and said, "Stay here with Jonathan, until I come back."

"Dusty," she said. "I have to admit, I'm a little scared."

He nodded. "That's good. In a time like this, you should be."

She said, "A time like this?"

He nodded. "This is war."

Dusty and Josh swung into the saddle and turned their horses toward the wooden bridge. As they rode away, Charles and Bree came out of the house and stood by Carter.

Carter said, "The Willbury's are in for a bad night. I wouldn't want them two boys riding down on me."

17

It was well past midnight when Josh and Dusty reined up. They were on what was called the Willbury Road, which led north out of Jubilee and after a while bent west, toward the Willbury Ranch. It was generally a two-hour ride from Jubilee to the ranch. Josh figured they were about a half hour from the main house.

"We should rest the horses," Josh said.

He swung out of the saddle and loosened the cinch. The horse he had chosen for himself was Rabbit. They were riding at night, and such a thing can be a little uncertain. He wanted a horse that was seasoned and knew the terrain, and yet was young enough still to have enough energy for the job.

Dusty was on a bay gelding that Bree had started calling Pinkie. Josh had no idea why. He thought sometimes she gave these horses cutesy names just to get under his and Josh's skin a little. Dusty dismounted and loosened the cinch. He had flipped his hat back and it was hanging by the rawhide thongs.

He said, "I've been thinking, maybe we shouldn't just ride up to their ranch. They're gonna be expecting us. Wouldn't you be?"

Josh nodded. "I suppose I would be."

"I think we should cut off the trail right now. Ride west through the hills for maybe a mile, then cut north. It's going to be slow going, but we should be able to approach their ranch house from the west."

Josh nodded. "Good having you along."

"Josh, just what is it you plan to do, once we're there? I can't see us hiding outside and shooting at the house. That's just not our way."

"I intend to deal with Kye Willbury face-to-face."

Dusty nodded. He looked off into the night. He looked like he wanted to say something, but wasn't.

"What?" Josh said.

Dusty looked at him with a little surprise. "Oh, nothing."

"Nothing my leg. What is it?"

"Well, Josh, it's just that we don't know for sure if it was Kye himself with those men tonight."

"We don't know that it wasn't. Besides, we know it was his men. Whether he was with them or not, he had to have given the orders."

Dusty nodded. "Maybe. Or maybe they were out here on their own."

"Do you think that's likely?"

"Well, Tom is sick, right? Kye's not really a leader, at least not from what I've seen."

Josh snorted a chuckle. "A leader? He can't even lead himself, much less others."

"And there's that husband of Genie's. What's his name?"

"Newt Wood. I don't know much about him. Seen him at Hunter's a few times."

"There could be a power struggle going on at the ranch. So, I guess what I'm saying is, go easy. Be subtle."

"I'm always subtle."

"That a fact?"

Josh was getting a little annoyed. "Yes, I'm always subtle. Stop grinning."

"I'm not grinning," Dusty said, trying not to grin.

"Yes, you are."

Josh tightened the cinch and climbed into the saddle. "While you're busy grinning, why don't you make yourself useful, and lead the way through these woods."

18

Josh and Dusty left their horses tethered behind a grove of pines, and emerged from the pine forest just beyond the Willbury bunkhouse. The moon was still up, and it was bright enough that they had a fair view of the grounds.

They crouched in the shadow of a ponderosa pine. The bunkhouse looked to be dark. Just beyond the bunkhouse and down a slight decline was a long, single-floor building, and there was a lamp burning in one window.

Dusty spoke low. He didn't whisper, because whispery sounds have a way of traveling on the night air. "That's the main house, with the lamp burning.

Josh drew his revolver and thumbed in a sixth cartridge. Dusty did the same.

Dusty said, "Now, remember. Go easy. Talk to Kye. Don't go in like a wild cat."

"I ain't no wild cat. Now, come on."

Dusty followed Josh down the decline. It was mostly dirt. He thought grass might have grown here at one time, but had been worn away by boot soles and horse hooves.

They stepped lightly up and onto a front porch. Josh didn't knock, but instead tried the door and found it unlocked. He swung it open and charged in.

Kye was standing just inside the doorway with a gun in his hand. Maybe he had been waiting for them, Dusty figured. Without a word, Josh drove his left fist into Kye's face, and Kye went down backward on the floor.

Dusty ran in behind Josh. He found the door opened onto a small parlor, and to one side, he saw Newt and Eugenia. Both were on their feet, and Newt was wearing a gun.

Dusty cocked his gun and aimed it at Newt,

bringing his arm out to full extension. "Leave that gun where it is."

Josh stood over Kye, with his gun aimed down at Kye's face.

Josh said, "Now, we're gonna talk about what happened at my house, tonight."

Dusty said, "I like it when you're subtle."

19

"Josh, Dusty," Eugenia said. "There ain't no need for this. Put away your guns. These two won't draw on you. I promise."

Newt nodded. "We'll do like she says."

Josh holstered his gun and let Kye get to his feet. Dusty slid his gun back into his holster.

"They told me what they done tonight," Eugenia said. "I'm so sorry for everything. I hope no one was hurt."

Josh said, "No one but your own man. The one who was on top of the roof earlier, aiming a rifle at us."

Eugenia looked at Kye. "You had a man aiming a rifle at him?"

Newt said, "Harmon. They got Harmon. They had a sharpshooter in a second floor window."

"That was Bree," Dusty said. "And she wasn't waiting for you. She went up there and picked him off. When you shoot at a house like that from out in the darkness, the flash of your gunshots tells people where you are."

"I suppose you would know that," Kye said, "since you're all gunfighters."

"Like I said," Eugenia said to him, "you shouldn't have ridden out there. Poor Harmon. He rode for Paw for a long time."

Dusty said, "We'll have the body delivered to you."

Josh said to Kye, "This has to stop. No more of it. My wife was in that house tonight, along with my sister. And my father's wife and their children. My little brother and my little sisters."

Kye was looking down toward his feet, but saying nothing. Dusty couldn't tell if Kye was embarrassed or furious.

Josh said, "If any of them had gotten hurt, then I wouldn't be standing here talking to you. Your sister would be burying you. Do you understand?"

Kye nodded, but he didn't look up.

Dusty looked at Newt and Eugenia. "I wasn't there tonight. Be glad of that."

Newt looked away from him. Dusty supposed no man likes to be made to feel small in front of his wife. But maybe it was what this man needed. Maybe feeling a little small right now would save his life later.

"Notice," Josh said, "we didn't come riding up here and shooting at the house. That's not what a man with any backbone does."

"Thank you," Eugenia said. "I'm so sorry for everything. If only these two would listen to reason."

Dusty said, "Maybe they will from now on."

Josh said, "We're gonna go out back and get our horses, and we're riding out. I'd appreciate it if no one takes any shots at us."

"They won't."

Josh looked at Eugenia and tipped his hat. "Sorry for the intrusion, Miss Genie. But, it's been that kind of night."

"No, *I'm* the one who's sorry," she said.

Josh turned and stepped out into the night, with Dusty behind him.

Newt drew his gun and took a few steps toward the door, but Kye held his hand up to stop him.

"Let them go," he said. "They've won this round."

Newt nodded reluctantly, and slid his gun back into its holster.

"Won this round?" Eugenia said. "What do you mean, won this round? The fight is over, Kye. Them two and the men who work for them, they could have attacked this house tonight and shot us all to pieces. We'd all be dead."

"Don't you never apologize for me again," he said.

"Kye, listen to me. I'm not saying you and Newt are bad men or not capable. You're stand-up men. Everyone knows that. You got nothing to prove. But you're not gunfighters. Those boys are. Dusty rode with outlaws, or so they say. Their father was a Texas Ranger. Even that sister of theirs—they say she killed a grizzly when she was only ten."

"Do you really believe all that?" Newt said.

Kye walked up to his sister. His red hair had fallen into his eyes, but he didn't bother to shake it away. His teeth were clenched together, and his lip curled a little like a cat that's snarling.

"Don't you never apologize for me again. You got that?"

For the first time in her life, Eugenia found herself afraid of her brother.

"All right, Kye. I didn't mean nothin' by it."

Kye went to the desk and slid open a drawer, and he pulled out a bottle of whiskey. There were two glasses on the desk, and he filled them both. Newt came over and took one glass.

"So, what now?" Eugenia said.

Newt gave his wife a look that said *are you serious?*

He said, "What now? What do you think?"

Eugenia was a little puzzled. "I guess I don't rightly know."

"I saw the way you looked at Josh McCabe."

She rolled her eyes with disbelief. "Newt, you can't be serious. I wasn't looking at him no special way."

Newt looked at Kye. Kye said, "I couldn't tell how she was looking at him. I was too busy getting punched in the face."

Josh's fist had caught him on the right eyebrow, and his eye was swelling shut and turning purple.

"Does that hurt?" Eugenia said. "Should I get a beef steak for it?"

"I don't want you touching me," Kye said.

"As far as I'm concerned," Newt said, "you're either with us in this, or you're with the McCabes. There ain't no middle ground."

He walked away from her and stood looking out a window, into the night.

Kye said to his sister, "I said at Paw's grave that if you can't stand with us, then maybe you should pack your things and ride out of here. I'm starting to think that's the best idea."

Eugenia's mouth fell open. "Kye?"

He said nothing more. He walked around behind the desk and sat in the chair. He put his feet up on one corner.

Eugenia looked at her husband. "Newt?"

He didn't look at her. "Maybe it'd be for the best."

"You want me to just ride out?"

He shrugged his shoulders.

"If I do, I'm takin' our daughter with me."

"Like I said, maybe it's for the best."

"First thing in the mornin'," Kye said, glancing at a grandfather clock that stood against one wall, "which will be in about two hours, looks like, I'd like you to have your things packed and be on your way. You can have the buggy. We won't be needing it."

"Go? Where will I go?"

He shrugged. "Not my concern."

Newt said, "I'm sure Josh McCabe will take you in."

She didn't know what to say.

Kye said, "Now, leave us alone. We have business to discuss. Ranch business. Business that don't concern you no more."

20

Eugenia was in a buggy with one horse pulling it along. She kept the horse to an easy trot as she approached town, then slowed it down to a walk as she rode onto Main Street. She had a floppy, wide-brimmed hat pulled down over her temples. It was really an old cowhand's hat, but it was all she had.

Her little girl was sitting on the wagon seat beside her. Red hair, like her mother's was tied into a braid, and she had a bonnet down over her head. Tucked in behind the seat were a couple of carpet bags, and a trunk.

She didn't know where to go. But she saw up ahead and to her left, a sign that read SECOND CHANCE. The restaurant and saloon owned by Miss Ginny and Mr. Hunter.

Partly on impulse, and partly because she didn't know what else to do, she turned the horse toward the building. She tugged on the reins so she stopped in front of the door on the restaurant side of the building.

Then she began to cry. She didn't realize the tears were coming, but they streamed down her face, and she broke out in sobs that she couldn't control.

She didn't even see the old Chinese man, on the porch with a broom in his hands.

"Miss?" he said. "You okay?"

At first, she didn't hear him.

He said it again. "Miss?"

She drew a shaky breath, and her sobs seemed to come under control. She wiped her eyes with both hands and said, "Is Miss Ginny in?"

"I get her. Wait here."

Within moments, Miss Ginny was coming out the door. "Eugenia, what happened?"

"He kicked me out. He done kicked me out."

"Who kicked you out?"

"My brother. My husband. Both of them."

A man was there, with a neatly cut mustache and goatee, which were both nearly white. He was in a checkered vest and a string tie, and he wore a gun at his side. Eugenia had heard Miss Ginny had married recently, and the man looked like a riverboat gambler. This must be him, she figured.

"Let me help you down," he said.

Once she was on the ground, she lifted her daughter down. She held her daughter's hand and let Ginny lead them into the restaurant.

"And who is this?" Ginny said.

"Miss Ginny, I'd like you to meet Rebecca. My darlin' daughter."

Ginny gave a grand smile. "Why, hello Miss Rebecca. It's a pleasure to meet you."

The girl was shy and maybe overwhelmed by everything going on. She clung to her mother's hand.

"Why don't you both come and sit," Ginny said.

All of the tables had red checkered table cloths, and Ginny led them to one and pulled out chairs for them. Ginny already had water hot for tea, so she poured a cup for Eugenia and one for herself. Sam fetched a glass of milk for Rebecca.

Eugenia took a sip. "Why, this is good. I have to say, I've never tasted tea like this. It's almost kinda flowery."

Ginny gave a little grin. "It's Earl Grey. The floweriness is from bergamot oil."

"Well, that there oil is mighty tasty."

Eugenia took another sip, then she set the cup down and told Ginny about the attack on the McCabe ranch house the night before, and the visit from Josh and Dusty.

"Oh, my," Ginny said.

Sam was in the room, straightening table cloths and such, getting ready for the day's business, and he heard what was said.

"I'll take the buggy to the livery and get some oats

for the horse," he said, "then I'll ride out to the house and make sure everyone's all right."

Ginny said, "Thanks, Sam."

Eugenia began rubbing her eyes. She looked so weary.

She said, "Miss Ginny, what am I gonna do? They kicked me out, and I don't have a penny to my name. Well, that ain't true. I got six cents in my pocket. But where will I stay? I got nowhere to go."

"As soon as you finish that tea, I'll walk over to the hotel with you. My credit is good in this town. Anything you need for Rebecca, we can get at Franklin's."

"But, Miss Ginny, I can't take charity. I just can't."

"Nonsense. I need a little help around here, sweeping up and serving tables. I was thinking about putting a *help wanted* sign in the window. Now I won't have to."

21

The following morning, Josh and Dusty had a table in the restaurant side of the Second Chance. Bree and Charles were with them.

The local tradition of morning coffee at Hunter's had evolved into morning coffee on the restaurant side of the business. Aunt Ginny had coffee going, both trail coffee and what she called civilized coffee. She had tea of various flavors, and some pie and biscuits.

Josh and the others rode in once a week or so for morning coffee. This morning would be the last one before spring round up. Josh had planned on starting the roundup today, but had delayed it a day on account of the ranch house being shot up.

A red checkered cloth was spread across the table, and there was a vase of tulips in the center.

Eugenia was in a white bib apron with ruffles at the edges. She came over with a kettle of coffee and said, "Anyone need a refill?"

Josh could use one, so she filled his cup, then she went on to the next table.

"I feel a little bad," Josh said. "I used to laugh at her and her brother. We never saw much of them, but when we did, they always struck me as awkward and kind of backward. But to be kicked out of your home like she was."

"Hard to believe old Tom is dead," Dusty said.

Bree took a sip of trail coffee. "I was serious the other night when I said she had a crush on you. At dances, she would just stand in the corner and watch you."

"And I never saw her," Josh said.

Dusty said, "None of this changes anything about the situation out at the stream."

"We're gonna need some of that range, and that stream is the only water supply for miles."

Charles said, "So, what're we gonna do?"

"I don't know. I kinda wish Pa was here. I could use his advice."

Dusty said, "He must be clear to the Jonas ranch, by now. Hopefully he's having an easier time than we are."

"I know one thing. When this roundup is done, I'm gonna put serious thought into hiring a full-time wrangler. Times like this, I want you at my side."

There was a noise from outside of hooves on the ground, iron-rimmed wheels turning on the gravel, and creaking springs.

"Must be the morning stage," Bree said.

Josh flagged Eugenia down for a slice of apple pie. Bree wanted a refill of coffee. And each sat with their own thoughts about what might happen if Kye Willbury tried to keep the McCabes from having access to the stream and the range on the McCabe side of it.

After a time, a man walked in. Josh knew him as Old Hank. He had been the stage driver around here since before Jubilee boomed its way into life, back when there was just a small collection of buildings that was called McCabe Gap.

Hank had a floppy hat and a white beard. He wore baggy pants tucked into tall, black riding boots, and he had a pistol on his belt.

"Hank," Josh said.

Dusty said his name and nodded toward him. Bree and Charles did, too.

Aunt Ginny walked over. "Good morning, Hank."

He touched the floppy brim of his hat. "'Mornin', Miss Ginny. Could sure use a cup of hot coffee before we continue on our way to Helena."

Ginny caught Eugenia's eye and waved her over. "Could you fetch a cup of coffee for Hank?"

"Sure can," she said.

Once Hank had a cup of coffee in one hand, he wandered over to the McCabe table.

"Boys," he said. "Miss Bree."

"Pull up a chair," Dusty said.

"Thanks, but no. Been sittin' on that hard, wooden seat all the way from Bozeman. I think I need to stand a while."

Josh was grinning. "We fully understand."

"What's new on the trail?" Dusty said.

"Oh, not much." He took a sip of coffee. "Word is some bad blood is buildin' between you and the Willbury's, though."

Bree said, "News travels fast."

"Kye Willbury and one of his men, a yahoo by the name of Newt Wood, were in Bozeman last night. They're hirin' gunfighters, Josh. Payin' 'em a cash advance. They're sayin' any McCabe riders come near the Twin Sister's stream, they're gonna shoot 'em out of the saddle."

Josh and Dusty looked at each other. Josh then realized Eugenia was in the room. He turned around his seat to try to find her. She was standing a few tables away, a kettle of coffee in hand, and she was staring at Josh. She had heard every word.

22

The sun wasn't yet in the sky as Dusty led his horse to the porch of the small cabin he and Haley called home. Dusty was in chaps and his old buckskin shirt. A dark blue bandana fell in the shape of a triangle across his chest. His gunbelt, the same one he had worn when he rode into this valley for the first time four years ago, was in place.

The porch had a single rail, and he gave the rein a couple of loose wraps around it. The horse was the tan gelding he liked, and that he called Pancho. He had named it before Bree could give it some silly name.

He stepped into the kitchen. A kettle of coffee was on the stove, and he poured a cup.

The coffee was hot, thick and black, just the way he liked it. He had taken a couple of sips when Haley came into the kitchen. She was fully dressed, and her hair was in a bun.

She said, "I don't like this. You riding out there into a potential range war."

He shrugged. "It's time for roundup. Has to be done. Anyone tries to stop us, we have to deal with it. It's the same on any ranch."

"I know. I just don't have to like it."

"I don't, either. I'm ready for it, but I don't like it."

He took another sip of coffee. "I got the wagon hitched for you."

She nodded. "As soon as Jonathan is up, I'll take him to the main house. We'll wait there until you're back."

"Bree will be there. Sam and Aunt Ginny will be there at night while we're gone, and so will Jack and Nina. Sam, Bree and Jack—they'll be able to handle any trouble that comes up."

"You've done this kind of thing before," she said. It wasn't a question.

He had told of his exploits before he came to Montana, but he figured she needed to hear about some of them again.

He said, "At the Cantrell Ranch in Arizona. We had to deal with rustlers a few different times. We had shootouts with them more'n once."

"But these are gunfighters that Kye Willbury has hired."

He grinned. "What do you think I am, sweetie?"

She nodded.

He said, "I hate to admit it. Sometimes I like to think of myself as just a cowhand. My old life is so far behind me. But I am what I am."

"I just want you to be careful."

"I will." He set his coffee down on the counter and pulled her into his arms. "Before, I was just fighting the fight that needed to be done. But now, I got something more to live for. You and Jonathan. I fully intend to fight for the ranch, but I also fully intend to come home."

She rested her head on his shoulder for a moment, and they stood in the kitchen in silence.

He said, "Old Ches is heading out this morning with the chuck wagon, and he has it full of rifles, and twice as much ammunition as he usually takes along. He's probably already started out. Josh and the men will be out there by noon. I hope to be already there with the remuda."

She nodded.

She walked with him out to his horse. He swung into the saddle.

"You be careful out there," she said with a smile. "I may be the granny woman now, but that doesn't mean I want to be pulling any bullets out of you."

"If the lead starts flying, I'll do my best to duck," he said with a grin. "I'll see you in a couple of weeks."

Josh had his own cup of coffee in his hand, and he stood on the porch watching morning come to life across the valley. Temperence stood beside him.

"Do you really think it'll come to shooting?" she said.

He shrugged. "Hard to say. Kye's not right in the head. That much is becoming more and more obvious. But to order a man to shoot at another, that takes gumption I don't know for sure that he has."

"He's done it twice already. And he was out here that night, helping out with the shooting."

"That's not quite the same thing. Those two cowhands who shot at me out by the Twin Sisters, that was little more than a pea shoot. And hiding out there in the darkness taking pot shots at a house, that was a cowardly thing. This time, he'll be ordering men to stand their ground and shoot at us. This time, it'll be full-on war. Takes some gumption and some backbone to do that."

"I hope he doesn't have the gumption."

He nodded. "Me too."

Charles stepped out. He was in his chaps and had his hat pulled down over his head.

"I'm thinking of saddling up and heading out. I told Kennedy and Taggart to be ready first thing in the morning."

Josh nodded. "I'll be right out behind you boys. Be careful. I don't want anyone going near the Twin Sisters stream until I'm there. But if trouble happens, you're in charge until I get there. Ches has ten rifles in that wagon, and boxes of ammunition."

Temperence said, "A rider's coming."

Josh looked out past the wooden bridge. Sunlight was touching the far ridges, but down toward the center of the valley everything was still immersed in the gray light of pre-dawn. Even still, he could see there was a single rider, following the trail that led to the bridge and from there to the ranch house.

He rode in a natural way, moving along like he and the horse were one. Every long-time cowhand Josh had ever seen rode like that. But something about this man said *gunfighter,* too. A fighting man moves a little differently than most men. He sits the saddle a little differently.

They watched as the man approached the house. He had a wide-brimmed hat that was pulled down, and his face was lost in shadow. He wore a pistol at his right side and a bandolier draped across his chest.

He reined up. Josh could see hair the color of straw dropping to his collar in back, and he had a beard that was graying.

"This the McCabe ranch?" he said.

Josh nodded. "This is the place."

"I just come from the Second Chance. They gave me directions. Is Johnny McCabe here?"

Josh shook his head. "Not at the moment. He'll be back in two or three weeks."

"My name is Scott Hansen. I used to ride for the Rangers with him, in Texas. A long time ago."

Josh nodded. "I've heard him mention the name."

"I was in Bozeman a couple of days ago. The Willbury ranch is hiring gunfighters. I thought it sounded like Johnny might need a little help."

Josh shook his head. "We're not hiring gunfighters."

"I'm not offering, either. But I am looking for work. I've been a cowhand on a couple different spreads in Texas. The King Ranch. The Shannon Ranch."

Josh nodded. "I've heard of 'em."

"Worked in Colorado for the Austin Ranch, near Denver, last summer."

"What brings you up this way?"

He shrugged. "Looking for a change of scenery. Thought I might say hello to my old friend Johnny. Then I heard about the Willbury ranch hiring gunfighters, and they're looking to shoot McCabes."

"Yeah, well," Josh reached up to rub the back of his neck, "that's a situation we're trying to nip in the bud."

Then he realized he hadn't introduced himself. "I'm Josh McCabe. I'm in charge. This here's my wife

Temperence, and my brother-in-law Charles."

Hansen nodded at them, and he touched the brim of his hat to Temperence.

Then something occurred to Josh. "You know something about horses?"

He nodded.

Josh said, "I'm looking to hire a wrangler."

"Wrangler?" Hansen looked a little surprised, and not in a good way. "I was hoping for a job as a cowhand, with full pay."

"My father has a different take on the job of wrangler."

For most ranches, a wrangler was a young man learning the cowpunching trade, or an older one whose bones were no longer up to long days in the saddle. But Johnny felt that a cowhand was only as good as the horse he rode. He wanted a top remuda, and a top hand to care for that remuda.

Josh explained it all to Hansen. He said, "On this ranch, wrangler is a top-paying job and considered one of the most important."

Josh had heard Pa speak highly of Hansen when he told of his old days with the Texas Rangers, and Josh had a gut feeling that Hansen was a good man. Pa had always said to trust your gut. And hiring Hansen as wrangler would free up Dusty.

Josh said, "The job is yours, if you want it. Fifteen dollars a month and keep."

Hansen nodded his head. "Wrangler, huh? Sure, why not."

Josh could see Dusty, approaching from off to the west.

Josh said, "That's my brother, Dusty, riding up now. He can show you the remuda."

23

Josh wrestled the calf down. He had both hands on the head and was twisting. The cow came down hard in the grass. Cowhands were cheering. Taggart was letting out some loud whoops. Zack Johnson was there, because his herd and the McCabe herd often used the same range. He called out, "Yeah, Josh!"

Josh hog-tied the calf, wrapping rope around the hooves fast, and then jumped up.

He said, "I'd like to see one of you yahoos top that!"

Dusty brought the branding iron over from the fire, the end of the iron glowing a dull red, and he marked the calf with the Circle M brand.

They were three days into the roundup. Josh had a tally book in his vest pocket. There were a number of new calves to be branded and castrated. It looked like the herd had grown by twenty percent over the winter.

Josh went to the chuck wagon for a cup of coffee. Ches had a huge fire going, and a pot of beans was hanging over it.

"Supper'll be ready in half an hour," he said to Josh.

He could hear the sound of bawling cows, and he could smell burned hair and hide.

Dust was in the air, and campfire smoke. And the rich smell of the beans over the fire, and coffee heating.

Dusty walked over and said, "Hey, Ches, is the coffee hot?"

"Always is," he said.

Dusty grabbed a tin cup, and Ches poured him a cup.

Josh said, "We had a good winter. The herd's growing nicely. Pa's gonna be pleased."

Dusty glanced over to a rope corral that was about five hundred feet from the chuck wagon. In the corral were the horses that made up the remuda.

He said, "Hansen is doing well with the wrangling duties."

Josh nodded. "Seems to be a good man. Pa always spoke highly of him."

"Boss!" Taggart called, running toward him. "Riders comin'! Looks like one's been hurt."

Josh dumped the rest of his coffee and followed Taggart. Dusty joined him.

One of the riders was Kennedy, and he was leading the other horse. Charles was on the second horse, and he was slumped over in the saddle, his right hand clamped around the opposite shoulder.

They reined up and Kennedy swung out of the saddle.

"What happened?" Josh said.

Kennedy said, "Charles has been shot."

Charles started to swing his right leg up and around the cantle, and Kennedy reached up to help him step down. Charles was in a faded gray shirt, but the shoulder of the shirt was soaking with red.

"How?" Josh said.

Charles was conscious, but in pain. "The Willburys."

"We didn't cross the stream," Kennedy said. "We done like you told us. We stayed on this side. But we were within sight of it, and they took a shot at us."

Charles said, "They had men positioned by the stream. They shot at us with a rifle. Fired a few times at us. One caught me."

Ches looked at the wound. "It ain't deep, but the bullet's in there. It's gotta come out."

Josh said, "You've treated wounds like this."

Ches looked at Josh. "But not here. And he's lost a lot of blood. He's gonna lose more when we get that bullet out."

Kennedy said, "There's a doctor in town."

Ches shook his head. "That one? Fresh from medical school, back East. Still wet behind the ears. He ain't likely seen anything like this."

Josh said, "How about Jack? He saved Carter's leg."

Ches nodded. "Maybe. If only we had Granny Tate."

Dusty said, "Haley can do this."

Josh looked at him. Josh wanted to say, *are you sure?* But he didn't want Dusty to think that he doubted Haley.

Charles said, "I'd trust Haley over that young kid doctor."

Ches cut a blanket into a long strip and wrapped it around the shoulder.

He said, "This will only hold for a little while, and it won't stop all of the bleedin'. And that's if he don't get jarred too much."

Josh said to Charles, "Can you ride?"

Charles nodded. "I think so."

Ches shook his head. "He ain't gonna make it. Too many miles, and the country is too rough. I'll get the buckboard."

Hansen hitched a team of two horses to the buckboard. Charles was strong enough to climb into the seat himself.

"Kennedy," Josh said. "Saddle up a fresh mount and ride back with them."

"If it's all the same, Boss," Kennedy said. "They took a shot at me, too. I want to be with you when you go after 'em."

"I only give an order once, Kennedy."

Kennedy nodded. "Yes, Boss."

Ches climbed up into the wagon seat beside Charles. Josh handed Ches a Winchester, and Ches leaned it against the seat between them.

"I don't expect trouble," Josh said, "but if anyone tries to stop you, shoot to kill."

Ches nodded. "I know what to do, Boss. Been through this kind of thing before."

Josh grinned. "I'm sure you have."

Kennedy rode up on a fresh horse.

Josh said, "Keep your eyes open."

Kennedy nodded.

Ches gave the reins a snap and a *giddyup* to the horses, and the team started forward.

Zack walked up to Josh. "Why'd you want Kennedy, specifically, to go along with them?"

"Because he got shot at, too. He'll be wanting blood. I'm hoping to get out of this with no more shots being fired."

"Do you really think that's gonna happen?"

Josh shook his head. "No."

Zack slapped him on the shoulder. "Hansen and I'll get fresh mounts for everyone."

Josh said, "Get the rifles out of the chuck wagon, too. I want every man with a rifle in his hand."

Dusty said to Josh, "It's gotta be said. What we do today, this is serious. We're making war. Nothing's ever gonna be the same again around here."

Josh looked at his brother. "Do you think I'm wrong?"

Dusty shook his head. "Riding on the Willburys is the only course of action we can take. If we don't, Kye'll think we're backing down."

Coyote Gomez was walking by. He said, "I think Kye Willbury has lost his mind."

Josh said, "I do wonder, myself."

Dusty nodded in agreement. "I just thought a few words should be said about the gravity of the situation. So we'll have it fresh in our minds while we go do what we gotta do."

Josh couldn't help but grin. "Gravity? You borrowin' some big words from Jack?"

Dusty returned the grin.

When the horses were ready, they mounted up. Zack had a Winchester in his hand, and Dusty was beside him with his Spencer.

Josh called out, "All right! Let's ride!"

24

Charles was stretched out on the sofa. Haley cut open his shirt around his shoulder to take a look at the wound.

Bree was nearby, with her hands over her mouth. Temperence had one arm around Bree's shoulders Jessica was standing with them.

Haley said, "He's lost a lot of blood, and the bullet is still in there."

Kennedy said, "They fired at us from a ways away. If we had been closer, the bullet would prob'ly have gone clean through."

Haley said, "I think we should send a rider into town for the doctor. He'll have the surgical skills necessary."

Charles shook his head. "No. He's fresh out of school. Younger'n I am. I don't want him touching me. I want you."

"But..," she had never taken a bullet out before.

But then she heard Granny Tate's voice in her mind. *You'll do fine, child. Trust yourself.*

Haley said, "Jack saved Mister Carter's leg, four years ago."

Temperence nodded. "But he hasn't touched a scalpel since then."

"I still want him assisting me."

Kennedy said, "I'll go saddle a horse and fetch him."

He ran out the front door.

Haley looked at the wound, and she thought about the time the summer before when she watched Granny take the bullet from the leg of a man who had been shot, one rowdy Saturday night when things had gotten out of hand at the Second Chance. The young doctor had been joining in the festivities and was too liquored-up to be of any good. Haley thought about everything she had read in Granny Tate's book about this kind of thing.

There was even a mention about the effect corn squeezings had on preventing infection. Granny had learned that from Pa. Haley glanced over to Pa's desk, and the carafe of scotch standing on it.

I can do this, she said to herself.

25

They reined up about five hundred feet from the stream. There was a small stand of alders near the water, and bushes, and a few scattered rocks. There were no men in view, and no sign of horses.

Dusty was to one side of Josh, and Zack to the other.

Dusty said, "Hard to tell, but it looks like they've pulled out."

Zack was squinting his eyes in the midday sun. "Seems they would have fired on us, by now."

Dusty said, "I want to go check it out."

Josh nodded. "Go."

Josh watched while Dusty turned his horse and cut a wide circle around the trees, then rode in from behind them. He rocks then pulled off his hat and waved at Josh and the men.

They rode on in.

Tracks covered the ground. Hoofs and boots. Cigarette butts were scattered about.

Taggart said, "Where do you suppose they went?"

Zack looked at Josh and said, "Back to their ranch."

Josh nodded. "That was what I was thinking. There are some areas between here and their ranch house that are better to defend than this place. I'll bet they're holing up at one of those places. And that's where we're heading to next."

They mounted up.

"We could follow their trail," Dusty said. "They didn't make any attempts to hide it. But we could be riding into a trap. Kye could have left men behind to take shots at us."

Josh said, "What do you suggest."

"If we're sure they're heading back to their ranch headquarters, maybe we should go there by a different route. Cut directly east, through the valley, and then onto Willbury Road, rather than go directly overland."

Josh looked at Zack, and Zack nodded.

Josh said, "All right. Let's go."

A road went directly north from the town of Jubilee. Some folks called it Helena Road, because it was the stage route to Helena, and some called it Valley Road. At one point, a road cut off from it, swinging east through McCabe Gap and into the valley. The same road that led to the wooden bridge in front of the McCabe ranch headquarters. That trail was called McCabe Road. But the main road continued on north and at that point was called Willbury Road by some. At one point there was a split, and a branch swung to the northwest and off toward the Willbury ranch house.

Josh, Dusty and the others cut across the valley, and then they picked up McCabe Road and followed it out to where it joined with Willbury Road.

The land about them, once they were out of the valley, was hilly and open, with large patches of juniper and various types of bushes. Jack could name them all, often using the Latin names, but to Dusty they were just scrub brush. Some looked a little like chaparral, though it didn't grow this far north. There were rocks and occasional stands of trees. One hill was gravelly and nothing grew on it but a few scattered clumps of grass.

In the distance, ahead and off to the right, were some tall ridges and peaks, looking sometimes blue and sometimes dark green in the distance. The Crazy Mountains. The valley was located in some ridges at the very southern tip of the Crazies.

They rode to where the road forked, and they took the northwest branch. The road cut through a wide gap between two ridges. It was in this gap that Tom Willbury had built his ranch house.

The land about them became more wooded as they approached the ridges. Ponderosa pines stood tall at either side of the trail.

Dusty saw a buckboard ahead of them, turned sideways in the road. Men were behind it. Barrels were standing by both ends of the wagon, giving men additional cover.

Dusty was about to point it out to Josh, but Josh already saw it and raised his hand for the men to rein up.

Kye Willbury called out to them, "That's far enough, Josh! Turn back!"

Josh called back, "Can't do that, Kye. You fired on my men. Hit one of 'em. My brother-in-law."

"Serves him right."

Josh wasn't sure if Kye meant because the riders shouldn't have been near the Twin Sisters, or because it was Charles who had married Bree.

Kye called out, "They was riding toward our land! I told you that's *our* land!"

Josh glanced at Dusty, then called out, "Is it worth dyin' for?"

That was when a shot was fired. No way to know which one of Kye's men had fired it. Could have been Kye himself. The bullet caught the brim of Zack's hat and sent it spinning away.

Josh tried to turn his horse, but it began rearing up. Dusty wasn't having much better luck. Zack leaped to the ground and dove behind the cover of a thick pine trunk.

More bullets were whizzing past them. A couple of shots kicked up dirt in front of them. Josh decided to leave his horse in mid-rearing and hit the ground running toward a pine across the trail from Zack. He lost his rifle somewhere along the way, but Dusty came to a sliding stop beside him on the pine straw and still had his Spencer in one hand.

Dusty brought the rifle to his shoulder and fired at the Willbury men. A deadfall was in front of the pine, so Josh took position there, kneeling, and fired with his pistol. A bullet tore off some tree bark near Dusty's head. He ducked back a bit, then jacked another round into his rifle and fired again.

As the Willbury men fired, Dusty could momentarily see a hat, or a shoulder with a rifle pushed up to it, and he would fire. Josh was shooting, the Willbury men were more than three hundred feet away. A difficult shot for a pistol. Josh's rifle was on the trail twenty feet away from him. No way he could run out to get it without getting himself shot.

Zack was at the other side of the trail, firing away with his Winchester. The other men were behind trees and a couple were behind a big rock, and they were all returning fire as well. Bullets were tearing away wood from the buckboard and the barrels in splintery strips.

One of the Willbury men yelped and fell back. But the firing continued. A heavy cloud of gun smoke was hanging overhead.

Dusty stepped around the tree trunk, away from the trail, and ran to another tree that brought him a little closer to the wagon.

He had a side view of one of the Willbury men. Not much to shoot at, just the side of a face and one shoulder.

Dusty brought the rifle to his shoulder. He had four shots left, if he had counted correctly. More cartridges were in his saddlebags, which were with his horse, and the horse had run off down the trail. Once the rifle was empty, he would have switch to his revolver.

He waited for the man to step fully into view. The man did, and Dusty was about to fire, but then he saw it was Kye. Dusty hesitated. To shoot Kye would change things between the Willburys and the McCabes forever.

"Josh!" he called back to his brother.

Josh backed away from the deadfall, moved around the back of the pine Dusty had been using at first, and then ran over to him.

Dusty said, "I had Kye in my sights. If I get him again, do you want me to take the shot?"

Josh looked at him and hesitated. Dusty knew it

was a serious question, and a hard decision to have to make. But that was what came with leadership.

Josh said, "Take it."

Dusty nodded.

He brought the rifle back to his shoulder and waited.

Kye stepped back into view. Just for a moment. But Dusty's rifle was cocked and he was as good a shot as Pa, and he pulled the trigger.

Kye went down.

A man called out, "Kye's been shot!"

Everyone behind the wagons and the barrels stopped firing. Josh looked back and raised his hand for his own men and Zack's to do the same.

"Kye!" a man called out. He stepped into view, running from one wagon to Kye. Dusty thought it was Newt Wood.

Josh looked at Dusty and Dusty nodded, and then Josh stepped out from behind the pine. Dusty brought his rifle up to give Josh cover, but the Willbury men were still holding their fire.

Dusty stepped out to join Josh, and then Zack left his cover at the other side of the trail and joined them, and the three began walking toward the wagons.

Dusty held his Spencer ready and Zack did the same with his Winchester, and Josh held his revolver in one hand. But there were no shots fired at them.

They stepped around the wagon, and saw Kye on the ground. Dusty's bullet had caught him in the side of the head, tearing away bone, and his hair was soaking with blood. His eyes were open but he was dead. Probably dead before he hit the ground, Dusty figured.

The Willbury riders were gathering around Kye, and Newt kneeling beside him.

"He's dead," Newt said. He looked up at Josh and Dusty, and said, "He's dead. Kye's dead."

Dusty thought he saw disbelief in Newt's eyes, and maybe a little fear. And maybe a little realization that this was not a game. That when you play with guns and try to start up a shooting match, the consequences can be deadly.

"What am I gonna tell Genie?" Newt said. Then tears began to roll down his face, and he started quivering. "You wasn't supposed to die, Kye! You wasn't supposed to die!"

Dusty thought Josh was about to say something. Maybe say you can't go shooting at a man without expecting you might get shot yourself.

But Josh slid his gun back into his holster, and he said nothing.

26

Kye was buried beside his father, behind the Willbury ranch house.

The day was cloudy, threatening rain. Aunt Ginny had brought a parasol with her, and so had Temperence. Josh stood with his hat in his hands. He wore a white shirt and a string tie, but his gun was still in place. Just to be on the safe side, he thought he should have a gun if he was going to be on Willbury land.

The grave had been filled in, and Eugenia was standing alone, staring down at it. Josh and the others were back a bit.

Dusty was with Josh. Haley and Jessica didn't come. They stayed back at the ranch with Charles and the children. Charles wanted to be there, but Haley didn't think he was well enough yet for riding. He had lost a lot of blood, and his recovery was going to be slow.

Bree was going to stay home with Charles, but he had insisted she come.

Jack was there, and Nina. Zack and his wife Crystal had ridden out from their end of the valley.

The Willbury hands were scattered about. Their hats were in their hands and they were looking toward the grave, but they were keeping their distance. Almost like they were afraid of Eugenia.

Josh decided maybe something should be said to her, and since Pa wasn't here, he felt the duty fell to him to speak for the family.

He stepped forward and said, "Eugenia, I'm very sorry about this whole thing."

Eugenia turned to face him, fury in her eyes. She said, "How could you let this happen?"

Josh was a little surprised. He said, "I didn't want this to happen. I tried to stop it."

"You're the gunfighter, Josh." She glanced toward

Dusty and Zack. "You're all gunfighters. Every man on both of your ranches is a gunfighter. Former Texas Rangers. Even outlaws." Her gaze landed on Bree. "Even you're a gunfighter. But Kye was just a cowhand. How could you let this happen? He's my only family. Mine and Rebecca's."

Josh said, "Eugenia..."

But he didn't really know what to say.

Eugenia raised a hand slapped him hard across the face. She said, "I didn't want a war between our families. But now, you've got one. Are you happy? I'm in charge, now. Hear me and hear me good—any rider of yours that sets one foot on that land by the stream, he'll be shot out of the saddle."

Eugenia turned and stormed away, past Ginny and the others, down toward the ranch house. Newt had been with the men, looking as afraid as all of them, but now he ran to catch up with her.

He said, "Genie? I'm still here. I'm still your family."

Eugenia turned sharply to face him. "I want you off this ranch, Newt. You don't belong here."

He backed up a step. "But, Genie. Little Rebecca, she's my daughter, too."

Eugenia looked over to the scattering of men, and called out, "Bower!"

The one called Bower came over. About thirty, with hair that was thinning in front, but a mustache that made up for it in thickness.

Josh thought Bower was no cowhand. He had been behind the wagons at the gun battle, and he wore his gun like he knew how to use it. Josh thought Bower might have been one of the gunfighters Kye hired in Bozeman.

Bower said, "Yes, 'm?

"This man is not welcome on this ranch. I want him gone by sunset. If you or your men see him on this land again, shoot him."

Newt said, "Shoot me? Genie?"

Bower said, "Yes'm."

He said it impassively. Just taking orders from the new boss. Shoot the man if he saw him again. All part of the job.

Eugenia walked away and into the house.

Bree said to Josh, "Are you all right?

Josh nodded his head, though his face still stung from where Eugenia had hit him.

He said, "Yeah. I've been hit harder."

He said to Dusty, "Why is it you shot Kye, but I'm the one who got hit?"

Dusty would normally have taken the opportunity to engage in some banter with Josh, but this time he only shrugged his shoulders. Josh gave him a nod, realizing this was probably not the time for banter.

Josh said, "I suppose I have only myself to blame."

Bree said, "Maybe we both do."

"If only we had taken them more seriously. Would it have hurt me to dance just one dance with Genie?"

Aunt Ginny said, "That's not why this happened."

Her gazed drifted down toward the house. "This happened because of a long road she has been walking, and that her brother walked alongside her. A lifetime of feeling small and inadequate."

Dusty said, "There was no need of it. They're as good as anyone."

Ginny nodded. "But sometimes, you have to hear it. You have to be told."

They began walking toward their horses, and the buggy Ginny rode in. They had all been left at the barn, across from the house.

Ginny said, "I didn't know Tom Willbury well. He seemed to be a strong man, and I thought maybe at times a stern one. But we knew so little of his family life. Of the life here, at his home."

Bree said, "They were here among us, and yet somehow alone and isolated."

Jack held Aunt Ginny's hand while she climbed

up and into the buggy. Sam and Hunter had both stayed back at the Second Chance, to run things while Ginny came to the burial. Jack and Nina had ridden with her. Once Nina was in place beside Aunt Ginny, Jack climbed up and took the reins.

Dusty swung up and into the saddle, and Bree and Jack did the same.

Josh took one last look at the Willbury house.

Bree said, "You coming, Josh?"

Josh nodded his head. "There's nothing more we can do here."

"I don't think there really ever was."

They turned their horses away and rode away.

27

Dusty and Josh left the ranch house as the sun was just beginning to show itself over the ridges to the east. They rode along, keeping their horses to a light trot. Josh was on Rabbit, and Dusty took Pancho.

They left the valley and rode east, through the foothills and toward the line cabin.

The roundup was over. Though they were a man short, and would be until Charles was again in the saddle, the rest of the roundup had been uneventful. Tallying the stock, branding the calves.

Dusty was once again working alongside Josh, now that they had a wrangler. Scott Hansen had worked out well during roundup and had stood alongside the men during the shooting match with the Willburys.

Josh and Dusty rode toward the Twin Sisters, and then reined up when they were about a thousand feet away. Dusty reached back and into his saddle bags for a pair of binoculars, and he trained them on the Sisters.

Dusty said, "She has men there. At least two, maybe more."

Josh nodded his head. He expected as much. He said nothing.

Dusty lowered the binoculars and looked at him. "So, what're we gonna do? Nothing's really been settled. That section of range belongs to this ranch, all the way up to the dry riverbed."

Josh sat in the saddle, looking toward the Sisters. He drew a long breath in, then let out slowly.

He said, "Let her have it. It's the least I can do."

Dusty gave Josh a long look, then he nodded.

Josh said, "I suppose there wasn't any need for us to ride out here. The floaters at the line cabin could have reported back to us. I just wanted to see it for myself."

"Josh," Dusty said. "None of this was your fault."

"I know that. At least in my head. But somehow, it doesn't feel that way."

Dusty gave his brother another long look but said nothing. He figured there was nothing more to be said.

"Come on," Josh said. "Let's get out of here."

They wheeled their horses around and rode away.

PART TWO

Thunder

28

It was Johnny's second morning on the trail that the snow started.

It came down lightly at first. A few flakes drifting by. The kind of snow Bree had always said was pretty. But by the afternoon, the wind picked up and the snow started coming down harder. It wasn't so pretty, now.

Johnny didn't want to go through the work of building a shelter in the snow. There had been a time when he cherished time in the mountains. He would have gone deep into the mountains, found the right spot, and built a lean-to where he would wait out the storm. He would have stood by a roaring fire with his coffee cup in hand and allowed the tranquility of the mountains to settle onto him.

But now he had Jessica in his life, and Cora and the twins. Now he had a reason to get this cattle-buying trip done and to get home. When Josh, Jack and Bree were young, it had been the same. So, with the snow coming down he rode into the small town of Dillon.

Johnny had been through Dillon a few years ago, and it had been little more than a crossroads with a saloon and a couple of houses. Now it had grown considerably.

He left Thunder at the livery.

"I'll give the horse some oats and rub him down," the old man running the livery said. His head was mostly bald, but he had a thick white beard.

"I wouldn't bother with the rub-down," Johnny said. "That stallion is only half-broke, and he can be ornery."

The man looked at Thunder, and Thunder gave him a loud snort. The man stepped back.

Johnny said to the old man running the livery, "You got a hotel in this town?"

"Oh, surely. The Corinne Hotel, just down the street."

With his bedroll under one arm, his saddle bags over his shoulder and his rifle in one hand, Johnny stepped out of the livery into the snow.

It was a hard snow, whipping past with the wind. Not unlike the storm that had hit the valley just before Christmas.

Johnny pushed through the wind to a long building that was three floors high, with Victorian molding around the top floor. There was a sign toward the top floor, but the snow cut down visibility and it was getting dark, so Johnny couldn't make it out. He figured it had to be the place.

"We got only two rooms left," the man behind the desk said. A thin man with a long thin nose, and with thin hair combed across the top of his head. "Due to the weather, all the stage passengers for the last two stage runs are here."

Johnny plunked the money down on the counter and got a room on the second floor. Johnny had been in the saddle all day and his joints were feeling a little rickety, and he didn't really feel like climbing the stairs. A sign of age, he supposed. But since heat rises, he at least wouldn't have to worry about being cold.

He left his gear in this room and headed downstairs for a meal. The dining room was full, but a waitress told him they would serve him in the bar.

He said, "Do you have steak and potatoes?"

She grinned. "Steak? Mister, this is cattle country."

So Johnny went to the bar to wait for his meal.

The bar went the full length of the room. Looked to be made of red oak, but sometimes that could be a little deceiving after finish was applied.

The last time Johnny was in Dillon, the only establishment of any kind had been a saloon with a dirt floor, and with a bar made of planks laid across upended beer kegs. Amazing what a little prosperity can do to an area.

There were men at the bar. A few Johnny figured to be travelers. A man in a dark gray suit jacket and matching trousers, and a black top hat. Another in a Boss of the Plains hat, but he was also in a suit jacket. But there were three who looked like cowhands, and a couple of miners. This might be cattle country, like the waitress said, but Dillon was largely a mining town.

It was the cowhands who caught Johnny's attention. One, in particular. He was in a gray range shirt and wore canvas pants the color of buckskin. His pant legs were tucked into riding boots that were black and rose to the knee. The man was large-boned, and his belly was swollen with fat. But it was the kind of fat you saw in powerful men. And Johnny recognized the way he stood, the slope of his shoulders.

The man had worked for Johnny at one time. In fact, he had been Johnny's top hand for a couple of years, until Josh had fired him.

Johnny decided to say nothing. He wanted no confrontation with him. He went to the other end of the bar.

The bartender had a waxed mustache that curled at either end, and a toothy grin.

"What'll you have, mister?"

Johnny didn't really feel like a drink, and he was still a little chilled from the ride through the storm.

He said, "Hot coffee, if you have any."

"I'll send over to the dining room for some."

Then Johnny heard the voice of the man he had seen at the bar.

"Well, there's a sight I never thought I'd see again."

Johnny glanced over. The man had moved away

from the bar.

Johnny said, "Reno. How have you been?"

Reno looked a little haggard. He needed a shave, and he looked noticeably aged since Johnny had last seen him. Too many years of hard drinking can do that to a man.

Reno said, "You got some nerve to talk to me. The way you fired me, after I been your top hand for so many years."

Johnny said, "You're the one who talked to me."

There were chuckles among the men at the bar.

Reno looked at them and had fury in his eyes. No man likes to be laughed at, Johnny thought, and it's even worse when he realizes they have something to laugh at.

Reno said, "Step away from that bar, McCabe."

Johnny did. He said, "Reno, you were fired from the ranch for disobeying orders."

"You weren't there to give orders."

"My son gave the orders. He was in charge while I was away. When I leave a man in charge, he speaks for me. To disobey him is to disobey me."

"I don't take no one's orders unless he earns my respect."

"He whupped your butt in a fight. As I remember it, you had a man with you. My son whupped both of you."

"That weren't the way of it!" Reno shouted. The desperate anger of a man who had been defeated in a war of words but didn't want to admit it.

"Then what way was it?"

Reno said nothing. His right hand was hovering near his gun.

Johnny said, "You have a strong back, and good skill with a horse and a rope. You were a good hand, when you were sober. Which you aren't, now. Go for that gun and it'll be the last thing you ever do."

The men scattered from the bar. Johnny heard one man say, "You know who that is?"

Another said, "I think that's Jim Austin."

Jim Austin, Johnny thought. A name that got mentioned from time to time. Good with a gun, and not one to be reckoned with. Austin was known to frequent the mountain towns from Idaho to Colorado.

A third man said, "No, that's Johnny McCabe."

Johnny said to Reno, "I mean it. Don't go for that gun."

Reno had never been the brightest man, and now he was liquored-up. Liquor has a way of making you stupid and brave.

Reno went for his gun. He wore it high on his hip, and he made a big, hasty motion in grabbing for it.

Johnny's gun came out in a clean, fluid motion. He cocked the gun as it came out, and his arm was fully extended with his gun pointed at Reno by the time Reno got his hand fully onto his own pistol.

The men in the saloon gasped.

Johnny said, "I don't want to have to kill you, Reno. Sober up, and you'll be an asset to any ranch in the area."

Reno was standing, staring wide-eyed at Johnny's pistol.

A man stepped into the barroom. A graying handle-bar mustache, a wide-brimmed hat, and a badge pinned to his shirt.

"By all the powers that be, can't a man have a dinner in peace without some yahoos wanting to shoot this bar apart?"

Johnny said, "Marshal, I'd appreciate if you'd get this man out of here before I have to hurt him."

"Reno," the lawman said. "You causin' trouble again?"

Reno cast his eyes downward.

The lawman walked over to him and held his hand out. "Give me your gun, Reno."

Reno pulled his revolver and handed it to him.

The lawman said, "Now I could march you down to the jail, but it's durned cold out and my dinner just got served. So I'm lettin' you off with a warnin' this time. Understand?"

Reno nodded. He said nothing.

Johnny released the hammer of his own gun and slid it back into his holster.

The lawman said to him, "You're new around here, ain't you?"

Johnny nodded. "I'm just on my way through to the cattle auction at the Jonas spread."

Johnny gave his name, and the lawman blinked.

He said, "You don't say. We don't often get a man as well-known as you around here. Jim Austin, from time to time. Luke Baker came through once. Shad Cain, too."

Johnny hated when this happened. It seemed to happen more and more, these days.

The marshal said, "Well, Mister McCabe. I'm sure Reno, here, won't cause you any more trouble."

"Thanks," Johnny said.

The lawman stepped back out to the dining room, and the men in the room burst into laughter. Reno fixed his eyes on the doorway and stormed out.

Johnny went to the bar and said, "Maybe I need something stronger than coffee, after all."

The bartender's grin was bigger than it had been when Johnny first walked in. "Anything you want, Mister McCabe. On the house."

One of the miners brought over a book that had a paper cover. The title at the top was AMERICAN NOVELS. On the cover was a drawing of a man in a ridiculously wide-brimmed hat with a gun in each hand. Below the drawing was, THE FIGHTING RANGER. And below that, *Johnny McCabe to the Rescue*. The price was ten cents.

Johnny's son Jack had been approached a few years ago by a writer from back East who wanted to write a dime novel about Johnny. Jack had said no, so the writer invented what he didn't know and wrote the novel anyway.

The man said, "Mister McCabe? Would you sign this for me?"

Johnny said to the bartender, "I definitely need something stronger."

29

The man sat at a table in a back corner of the barroom. He had arrived on the stage and was heading to points west. Or so he had said. A writer, here from a newspaper back east. New York, if you must know. He was here to write about the west.

He wore a wide-brimmed hat, and was in a jacket and tie. Inside the jacket, in a specially made holster, was a Smith & Wesson .44. And tucked into the back of his jacket, just beneath the collar, was a dagger in a specially made sheath. He could reach behind his neck, grab the dagger and have it flying through the air and into a target faster than you could talk about it.

Beneath his shirt was solid muscle. When he moved, he did so with grace and finesse.

In front of him was a meal of veal cutlets, and a snifter of brandy. He was having his meal in the barroom, because the dining room was full. He didn't mind. He didn't like crowded rooms. He liked rooms like this one, where he could keep his eye on everyone present. In a room that was too crowded, it might be possible to miss someone. And an omission like that could get you very dead, very quickly.

He was good at what he did. And what he did was not writing for a New York newspaper. He made his living hunting men and killing them.

He was paid a lot for his services. He was no two-bit bounty hunter, but a man whose services were sought throughout the world. Europe, South America. And here in this country.

The only man in the room he felt might be on his level was the one at the bar. The one who had just drawn on the drunken cowhand. The one who could have killed the drunken cowhand if he had chosen to.

A mistake, the man thought. The drunken cowhand was going to kill the gunman, or force the gunman to kill him. When a man is trying to kill you, sparing his life might seem charitable, but it was really just delaying the inevitable.

There weren't many men as good with a gun as the man at the bar. But the man at the table wasn't going to waste his time guessing.

The waiter came over and said, "Is everything all right, Mister Brown?"

The man was going by the name Brown at the moment. He said, "Yes, everything's fine."

Then he said, "The man at the bar, who is so good with his gun. What might his name be?"

The waiter was of African descent, and he broke into a broad smile. "Why, that's Johnny McCabe. The famous gunfighter."

The man calling himself Brown nodded. He wasn't surprised.

He reached into his jacket, pulled out a silver dollar, and set it down on the table.

He said, "I'm a writer from New York."

"Yes, sir. I've heard talk."

The man smiled. He supposed they didn't get big-city writers from New York all the way out here very often.

He said, "I need you to keep your ear out. I'm here searching for a man."

"For a whole dollar?"

"No," Brown said. He set down a second dollar. "For two."

The waiter was ecstatic. In these frontier towns, where a cowhand often made less than twenty dollars per month, and miners even less than that, where five cents could buy you a mug of beer and ten cents a half hour with a harlot, two dollars was an exorbitant tip.

"There's a man by the name of Jeb Jones. An old frontiersman. At times a wagon train scout. I'm looking to interview him, for the newspaper back East."

"I'll spread the word, sir."

For two whole dollars, the waiter didn't just keep

his proverbial ear open. He asked questions. First the bartender. Then the livery stable hostler, when the man came in for a drink. Also the head waiter.

Within an hour, the waiter was back at the table. "They say a man with that name has a cabin somewhere in the hills outside of town. They don't know just where."

"Do they know how far?"

The waiter shook his head. "No, sir. But the head waiter don't think it's more than a day or so out. The man you're looking for has been in this very barroom more than once. Not for a while, though."

Brown smiled. "Thank you very much."

"If there's anything else you might need, all you have to do is ask."

Funny, Brown thought, how money can buy you courtesy.

Johnny McCabe was leaning one elbow on the bar. His left elbow, so his gun hand could be free. He had decided to go with beer, and his mug was nearly empty.

The bartender came on over. "I just got word from the kitchen. Your meal should be ready soon."

Johnny nodded his head in acknowledgement, but his eyes were on the man from the corner table. The man placed his hat on his head and walked out the door to the corridor beyond. Johnny couldn't help but notice the way he walked. Not dropping each foot down, but placing it down. His boot heels made little sound as they touched the floorboards.

Johnny said, "Who was that man?"

"Why, that was Theodore Brown. He's a writer from a newspaper in New York. Out here to do a story on a local scout and mountain man."

Johnny kept his eyes on the doorway a moment, then looked back to the bartender.

Johnny said, "I don't know just where that man's from, but he's no writer for a newspaper."

30

Her name was Melissa Jean, and she was fifteen years old. She felt like an old fifteen, with all she had seen. Her hair was a light blonde. Her daddy had said it was the color of summer sunshine, and the memory of him saying that brought a smile. But he was no longer on this Earth and she would never hear him say it again.

It was late spring in the mountains of Idaho Territory. Late spring, but it still felt like winter.

She and Eli lived in a single-room house—more of a shack really. The walls were made of logs. Some of the mud was falling out from between the logs, and the cold winds could slip in at night. But there was a cliff on one side and a stand of tall pines on the other, and most of the winter winds didn't make their way to the cabin.

A pot-bellied stove stood by one wall, and a fire was roaring in it. Kept you tolerably warm, as long as you wore a sweater.

Eli was twelve years old, with black hair that grew in tight curls if he let it grow long enough, but he usually kept it cut close to his scalp. His skin was the color of chocolate.

He said, "How soon will that stew be ready, Missy?"

Beef stew. A cow had drifted its way in toward the cabin couple of weeks ago. A stray from one of the ranches outside of Dillon. Missy had slaughtered it herself.

She said, "Won't be long. Just you be patient."

"I'm not good at being patient."

Melissa Jean had to grin. "You know what you could do instead of pacing around in here and being impatient?"

"What?"

"Go out and get me some more firewood."

Eli gave her a slack-shouldered, mouth-open kind

of look. Like using the whole body to sigh with exasperation. Something all kids seemed to be masters at.

"You know how cold it is out there. You don't want it to get cold in here, do you?"

"Eli, what're we gonna do when the firewood runs out?"

Eli grinned and got to his feet. "I'm just funnin' you. I'll get the wood."

He was right about letting the cold in. When he opened the door, a cold gust shot across the room.

He came back a few moments later with an armload of wood and dropped it into a wood box by the stove.

He said, "Winter is almost over. The snow has already stopped, and by tomorrow it'll feel like spring again."

"You sure?"

Eli nodded. "I'm sure. And once spring has fully set in, I'll see about going about and cutting us some firewood for next winter."

"Maybe I can help."

He raised his brows and gave her a look that said, *you're not serious.*

He said, "You can hardly lift the axe. You're just a little wisp of a girl."

She pulled herself up as tall as she could, which wasn't very tall. "I'm no wisp."

"Well, you sure ain't very big. You tend to the cabin, and I'll tend to the firewood."

He headed outside for another armload.

Melissa Jean gave a weary sigh. She put on a smile for Eli, and it was true that with the help of Mr. Jones, they had found a way around every problem. This was his cabin. But Mr. Jones was very old. What would happen when he was gone? Or if the people they were running from found them?

She pushed a spoon into the stew and gave it a stir.

31

Johnny waited out the cold spell. He had lived a long time in these mountains, and cold spells in June didn't usually last long. He was right. By his second day in Dillon, the sky was blue and the snow that had drifted against the buildings and covered the boardwalks was gone. The street was wet with run-off and you could sink to your ankles in the mud.

He stepped out of the hotel and took a deep inhale of the air. He could smell balsam, and the deep earthen smells that come from wet ground.

He was in his jacket, and he had his saddlebags over one shoulder, his bedroll tucked under one arm, and his rifle.

He figured he was maybe a day and a half out of the Salmon River country. Because of the snow cover, if he wanted to make good time he would have to take the trails.

The marshal came walking along. Johnny had learned his name was Brantley.

"So, Mister McCabe," Brantley said. "Are you leaving us?"

Johnny nodded. "Have to be riding on."

"Well, we enjoyed having you here. It's not often we get a living legend in our fair city."

Johnny shook the man's hand. But he wished the man would stop talking like that.

The man said, "You're about the most famous man I ever met. I met Bass Reeves once, down in the Nations. He's a deputy marshal, now. Makin' quite a name for himself."

Johnny nodded. He had heard the name.

Johnny made his way down the boardwalk. The livery was on the same side of the street, so he wouldn't have to walk through the mud.

As he walked along, he started to seriously think

about using an alias when he traveled. The name *Reynolds* had worked for him, years ago. Maybe he should try it again.

Reno had waited out the storm and then returned to the ranch, only to find the ramrod waiting for him.

The ramrod was a tall man, with a black hat and a red shirt. He said, "We heard about what happened in town. Getting yourself drunk and almost shot. Trying to draw on a man like Johnny McCabe. If even half of what they say about him is true, it would have been suicide. You made the ranch look bad."

"I'm sorry, Boss. Won't happen again."

The man shook his head. "Won't happen again here. Go to the main house and pick up your pay. I don't want to see you again on this ranch."

And so Reno found himself riding along a ridge with fourteen dollars in his pocket and no job prospects.

It had all began when McCabe's boy fired him, Reno thought. His life had gone downhill since then. The McCabe name was like gold. Most people wouldn't hire him once they found out he had been fired from the McCabe ranch. He lied once and told a ramrod he had quit the McCabes, telling him it had just been time to ride on. But after a couple of months, the ramrod had learned the truth and fired him. Reno had to ride all the way to Idaho Territory to find a job. And now that job was gone, too, and it was also because of Johnny McCabe.

The snow was melting fast. The temperatures had to be in the sixties, and the sun was warm on his shoulders.

He was wearing a canvas jacket that was lined with sheepskin, and he pulled it off. He reached back to shove the jacket into one saddle bag, but then he thought about what was in that saddle bag and pulled it out. A metal flask.

He pulled the cork and took a pull. Whiskey, which he kept on hand for an emergency.

So, where to head for from here? South to the Cheyenne area. Maybe Medicine Bow or Laramie.

He pushed the cork into the flask, and he saw motion down below. A trail cut through a depression that was almost a gully, beginning at the foot of this ridge. The ridge wasn't very high, and Reno could see the rider clearly enough that he blinked with surprise when he recognized who it was.

Danged if it ain't Johnny McCabe, he thought. Out here, all by his lonesome, just riding along. Old high and mighty Johnny McCabe.

Well, out here in the mountains, Reno thought, *you ain't no better'n I am.*

Reno found fury rising up in him. McCabe had made him look small, two nights ago. McCabe had made him look small more than once, back when Reno worked for him.

Reno shoved the flask back into his saddle bags, and then slid his rifle from the scabbard.

It was an old Winchester yellow boy. Almost twenty years old, but it still fired.

He jacked a round into the chamber, working the action slowly and hoping the sound didn't carry.

McCabe continued to ride along. Must not have heard.

The trail down below was maybe three hundred feet away. McCabe was a hundred or so feet further along. Four hundred feet. Could Reno make the shot?

When he was younger, he had been a good shot with a rifle. But now he was nearly forty and his hands shook a little from too much drink over the years.

He sighted in on Johnny. He surely hoped his shot was good, because if he missed, there was no way the nag he was on could outrun that mountain stallion of McCabe's.

Reno pulled the trigger, and McCabe fell from the saddle.

By gum, Reno thought. *I done it. I killed Johnny McCabe.*

32

"But what if he ain't dead?" Reno said aloud, as though his horse could understand him. "That Johnny McCabe is the dang luckiest sumbitch I ever did meet."

Johnny was lying face down on the ground. His hat had fallen away as he fell, and his mountain stallion had run off.

Only one way to tell, Reno thought. He hated the idea of going down there. If McCabe wasn't dead, if he was just lying there playing possum, then Reno knew he himself would be a dead man. Even if he just rode away, McCabe could track him down.

One thing was true, Reno had never met the man who could get the best of McCabe in a gunfight. Reno had been a fool to try back in Dillon, but it had been because of the whiskey.

He sat in the saddle a moment longer, dreading what he had to do. Ride down there and see if McCabe was dead.

He thought for a moment about how his name would spread. The man who killed Johnny McCabe. Brought a little grin to his face. Then his name would be spoken with respect.

But then he realized McCabe's sons would be coming after him. All three of them. Not only that Josh boy, but the other two. And maybe Zack Johnson.

Reno decided he wouldn't tell anyone about the shooting. He would ride down the slope, make sure McCabe was done, then just ride on out of there.

He reached back for that whiskey flask again. He needed one more drink. He pulled the cork and took a mouthful, then pushed the flask back into the saddle bags.

He jacked another round into the rifle. He wasn't foolish. He wasn't about to ride up onto McCabe without having a round chambered and the rifle cocked.

Reno had been working in this area since the spring before. He knew the slope leveled out a bit a quarter mile on, so he clicked his horse forward.

There was still snow in places, and it was slushy. The slope was sandy and the sand was wet. The hooves of the horse sunk entirely in a couple of places, but the horse kept its footing and continued on.

The ground at the foot of the low slope was somewhat flat. There were puddles here and there, and in shady spots snow was hanging on.

Reno clicked his horse ahead. McCabe was still lying face down in the mud.

Reno noticed McCabe's stallion a hundred yards away, standing and watching him. He thought little of it, and returned his eyes to McCabe.

Them McCabes can be sneaky, Reno thought. It would be just like him to suddenly roll over with a pistol in his hand and begin blazing away.

Reno had his rifle ready. One move from McCabe, and Reno would put a bullet in him. He reined up twenty feet from McCabe. Still, the man wasn't moving.

Maybe he's dead after all, Reno thought. Serves him right.

Reno swung out of the saddle, holding his rifle in his right hand, gripping it like a pistol. Finger on the trigger.

He walked over to McCabe. Reno wasn't sure if he was breathing.

He kicked McCabe in the ribs. Once. Twice. No response.

Then he heard a sort of roaring sound, and he looked up to see the stallion almost on top of him.

He yelled out as the front hooves began clawing at him. His rifle went off and then was knocked from his hand.

Reno yelled again and tried to back away, but the horse was attacking. A hoof caught him above one eye, and another one on the shoulder.

Reno was knocked to the ground and the horse

was on top of him. Jumping on him. Crushing. Stomping.

Reno called out for help, but there was no one to hear him.

33

Thunder lowered his head and pushed at Johnny with his nose. Once, then twice.

Johnny didn't move.

Thunder walked around Johnny in a circle, then stopped and looked at him. Then Thunder nudged him with his nose again.

Johnny stirred.

Johnny lifted his head. Blood soaked the right side of his hair and had made a stain on the shoulder of his jacket.

"Thunder?" Johnny said.

Johnny grabbed one stirrup with an unsteady hand and tried to pull himself to his feet. His legs weren't strong enough and he went back down onto the sand. Then he tried again. Grabbing the stirrup and pulling.

He got so he was partially standing, enough so with one hand on the stirrup, he could reach with the other to the saddle horn.

He pulled some more until he was fully upright. His knees were wobbly and his head pounded.

He lifted a foot to the stirrup, but had to steady the stirrup with one hand so he could slide a foot into it. Then he stepped up and swung his leg partly over the back of the saddle. He fell forward in the saddle, his head resting against the back of Thunder's neck, and he lost consciousness again.

Thunder turned and started out of the canyon.

Reno lay in the sand, blood soaking his hair and the front of his shirt.

The day was warm and the snow was melting. Johnny rose to consciousness once and realized he was on the back of Thunder. He knew it was Thunder, because of the way the horse moved. Each horse moved in its own unique way, just like a human.

He felt foggy. Like back in the days when he would indulge in too much tequila. Everything seemed to be swimming about him.

He blinked his eyes and brought things into focus. He saw pine trees, and the land seemed to go upward at an angle.

This is the side of a ridge, he realized. He was in the mountains.

Then he passed out again.

Thunder continued along, climbing the ridge. Then he started down the other side.

He walked carefully. His left front shoe had come loose when he kicked at Reno. It hurt when he stepped down.

He came to a stream and pushed his muzzle into it.

After a few mouthfuls of water, the horse stepped into the stream. The cold water felt good on his hoof.

He began walking through the water, following the stream.

Eli drew in a deep lungful of air. He was in a plaid shirt with suspenders over his shoulders, and he was enjoying the feeling of warm sunlight on his face.

He said, "This is it, Missy. I feel it. The last snow."

"That's what you said after the last snow." Melissa Jean was pinning wet laundry to a line strung from the wall of the cabin to a pine tree thirty feet away.

Eli nodded. "I know. But I'm right, this time. I can really, really, really feel it."

"And it's *Melissa Jean*, not *Missy*."

He gave her a look. "What you talking about? The whole time we been growing up, you always been *Missy*."

She pushed her chin out indignantly. "Well, not anymore. I'm near grown to a woman now, and I should be called *Melissa Jean*. It's what Momma called me."

"And here I thought you were just being uppity

again."

"I am not uppity."

There were sections of snow a few inches deep, here and there. But it was a soft, slushy snow. Melting fast.

Melissa Jean said, "Why don't you help me with the laundry?"

Eli didn't say anything.

Melissa Jean said, "Eli?"

He said, "Missy? Get over here."

His voice sounded urgent. A little scared.

Melissa Jean looked up from the laundry, and followed Eli's gaze. He was looking off toward a line of pines beyond the cabin.

A rider was approaching, but he wasn't sitting in the saddle like a rider usually does. He was slumping forward against the horse's neck. He didn't have a hat, and Melissa Jean wasn't sure he was even awake.

"Wait here," Eli said, and he ran to meet the horse.

"Eli," she said. "Get back here."

She knew Eli was trying hard to be a man. Trying to take care of things. But he was only twelve.

"Mister?" Eli said.

Eli grabbed at the reins, but the horse turned its head away and took a couple of steps away from Eli.

Then the man fell to one side and landed in the mud.

He was in a brown waist-length jacket and wore his gun like he knew how to use it.

Eli saw there was blood in his hair and down the side of his face.

Melissa Jean ran up beside him. He said, "Missy? Is he dead?"

"No. He's breathing. But he's hurt bad."

"What're we gonna do?"

"Hush yourself. Let me think a minute."

This was bad, Melissa Jean thought. She couldn't just let him lie out here in the mud and die. If she got him back in the saddle and sent him on his way, he would just fall out of the saddle somewheres else and probably die there.

The man needed a doctor, she thought. They weren't far from the town of Dillon. Maybe a few hours. But as far as Melissa Jean knew, no one knew she and Eli were here. It would be better for them if that's the way it stayed.

She wasn't about to let them be found. They had worked too hard to get as far as they had gotten. But she couldn't just let this man die here, either.

She looked off toward the trees at the base of the cliff the cabin faced. Mr. Jones had ridden off that morning to hunt and said he would be back by nightfall. She realized she and Eli were going to have to handle this themselves.

She said, "Come on, Eli. Help me get him into the cabin."

34

Theodore Brown had a room on the second floor of the Corinne Hotel. He watched the street below as Johnny McCabe rode along the street.

McCabe rode like he was born to be on the back of a horse, Brown thought. And Brown noted how he rode, with his right hand within reach of his gun.

It was morning, and it looked like the trails might be passable. Brown had work to do.

He thought McCabe had the right idea. Horseback was the way to approach the job ahead of him.

He had been hired to find Jeb Jones. Not that he necessarily needed Jones, but some information Jones would have.

Brown had arrived in town as a dapper gentleman. But where he was going, such a man would be out of place. He went to his bag and pulled out jeans, a buckskin jacket and a gunbelt.

His next stop would be the livery to purchase a horse and saddle. And then to a general store and a gunsmith. He would need supplies for the trail, and he would need a rifle.

Brown, of course, was not his real name. He had used many names over the years, but he hadn't used his real name in a long time. He no longer even thought of that name as belonging to him.

Once he finished what he had to do, he would be discarding the name Brown and going on to his next job.

This job struck him as distasteful, but he was being well paid. More than a cowhand could hope to make in three lifetimes. A good thing, because the man had an expensive lifestyle.

His employers wanted two children killed, but only after they gave him certain information his employers wanted. If what Brown had learned was correct, the children were with Jeb Jones, or Jones would know where they were.

There was one concern in all of this. There always was. Something that kept the job from going smoothly. In this case, it would be the name Jim Austin. The gunfighter and scout. The consistent talk was that Jeb Jones was a close friend of Austin's. Apparently Austin considered him family. Something about a wagon train years ago. Austin had been a young man and Jones was their scout.

When Johnny McCabe had walked into the barroom of the Corinne Hotel a couple of nights ago, the man called Brown figured him to be one of just four men. Considering the area and its proximity to Bozeman and the boom town of Jubilee, he knew it could very well be McCabe himself. It might also be Robert "Gray Eagle" McAllister. A third possibility was Shad Cain. A fourth was Jim Austin.

Brown didn't want a run-in with any of them. Brown wasn't afraid of these men, because he knew he was a fighter on their level. But he also wasn't getting paid to fight that kind of man. He didn't fight out of anger, or to make a point, or even for honor. If he was to engage a man who might defeat him, there had to be money in it. And to engage McCabe, McAllister, Cain or Austin, it would have to be a lot of money.

He rode the trail out of town. Snow was still on the ground to either side of the trail, but the trail itself was clear. Muddy, but devoid of snow.

He followed along for a while. He wasn't sure what he was looking for. Just riding along to see what he might find. Any sort of clue that might lead him along to another clue that might eventually lead him to the cabin of Jeb Jones.

He was a few miles out of town when he saw a horse approaching. The animal had a saddle but no rider.

The horse stopped and Brown rode up to it.

He took the reins.

He knew it was not the horse Johnny McCabe had ridden from town. McCabe had been on a magnificent stallion. Brown knew horseflesh, and it was hard not to notice the stallion.

"Well, boy," he said. "Now, what happened to you? Throw your rider?"

He had spoken with an accent that had the rhythm and melodic sound of the British. His true accent. He could copy many different accents, and while in town he had been using the accent of the gentile in Boston.

He realized how foolish it was to talk to a horse, because one had never answered him back. Still, it was something a man who spent too much time alone started doing. The profession Brown followed had taken him all over the world. He had hunted men in the Andes, and across the savannas of Africa. One thing many of these hunts had in common was extended time alone.

He took the horse by one rein and continued along, leading it.

He came to a flat area near a ridge. The land was muddy and sandy, and lying in the sand was a man. Brown recognized him as the drunken cowhand who had been foolish enough to challenge McCabe. The cowhand looked like he had been trampled. Torn flesh all about his face. Looked like one cheekbone might be crushed. A leg was twisted at an uncomfortable angle. Blood soaked the man's shirt and had puddled beneath his head and shoulders.

"What on Earth happened to you?" Brown said.

He swung out of the saddle and left both reins trailing. He checked the body for a pulse or any signs of breathing, and he found the cowhand wouldn't be answering any questions. Ever.

What could possibly have happened here? Tracks were scattered about. Brown knew how to track—one of the skills of his job. He stood and took a good look at the tracks in the sand and mud, and let them tell him their story.

There had been two riders. One riding along. Brown found where the rider had fallen from the saddle. A dark patch of mud where the rider had landed told him there was a wound. Possibly, he was shot from the saddle.

Then a second rider approached from the nearby ridge. Tracks from the first horse stretched off a few hundred feet, so he figured the horse had wandered a bit.

Then the second rider had dismounted. And then, if Brown was reading the tracks correctly, it looked like the horse of the first rider had attacked the second rider. The second rider being the now-dead cowhand.

The tracks were smudged in places. Very seldom when people are going about their lives do they think to leave clearly defined footprints in the dirt.

It appeared that after the first horse had attacked the cowhand, the horse's former rider climbed back into the saddle, and they started off.

Brown swung back into the saddle and backtracked the second horse to the ridge.

The slope wasn't very severe, and even though the horse he had bought from the livery wasn't mountain-bred, it could handle the climb.

Brown found where the horse had stood atop the ridge. He had a view of the dead cowhand, down below.

Then it dawned on him.

"Well, blow me down," he said with a smile, not bothering to cover his British. "You shot the first rider, from up here. You aimed at him with a rifle, shot him out of the saddle, then rode down to check on him. And then, if I'm reading the tracks properly, the rider's horse attacked you and trampled you to death."

Then another thought occurred to him.

"McCabe," he said. "The man you shot was McCabe. The man who had humiliated you at the saloon, two nights ago."

There was nothing to indicate the first rider had

been Johnny McCabe. But much of Brown' profession involved the same skills as a detective. And much of a detective's work involved gut feeling. If you focused only on clues and tried to sort out the puzzle, you would never have the whole picture.

The first horse seemed to move off down the trail. Brown thought he might follow the trail for a while. See what he found.

35

Eli said, "I really think we should go into Dillon and get a doctor. There must be one there."

Melissa Jean shook her head. "We can't take the chance. You know that. You know what'll happen if they find us. The people who're looking for us. We'll wait for Mister Jones to come back."

Johnny was stretched out on a bunk, and his head was wrapped in a torn bedsheet.

Melissa Jean said, "We washed out the wound, and I stitched it up best I could. I remember watching Momma do it."

"What do you suppose happened to him?"

Melissa Jean shook her head. "Don't know. Could'a been anything, I guess. We just have to wait till he wakes up."

The cabin had one room, and the rear half of it was separated with a blanket that was tacked to the ceiling. Behind the blanket were bunk beds, and Johnny was in the bottom one.

Eli said, "What do we do about that gun?"

Johnny's gunbelt was still in place.

Eli said, "We shouldn't just leave it on him, should we?"

"I'm not touching it. I don't know anything about guns."

"What if he's an outlaw? What do we do?"

"Right now, what we're gonna do is sit down for supper. We'll figure everything else out later."

They ate, and then Melissa Jean pulled the blanket back to check on their patient. His eyes were fluttering open. He was waking up.

"Mister?" she said.

Johnny blinked his eyes a few times. He said, "What happened? Where am I?"

"You're here in our cabin," Eli said. "Well, it ain't ours, but we're using it."

Melissa Jean said, "You rode in with a huge gash on your head. I treated it best I could."

"My horse," Johnny said. "You've gotta be careful of him. He's a half-broken stallion and doesn't like strangers touching him."

She shrugged. "I led him into the stable we have and took off the saddle. He was real gentle with me."

Johnny couldn't help but smile. "Well, Thunder's always been a good judge of character."

He went to sit up.

She said, "You might not want to do that, yet."

Johnny's head was swimming, and he lay back down. "I think you're right."

Eli said, "Just who are you, Mister? What's your name?"

"Johnny McCabe," he said. "My family owns a ranch about a day's ride northeast of Dillon. I was on my way to a cattle auction down in the Salmon River country. Looks like I'm not gonna make it there in time."

"What happened to you?"

He squinted a little. "I don't rightly remember. I remember being in Dillon. I waited out the last snowfall there. Then I was heading out. And that's all I remember."

He reached up to touch his head.

Melissa Jean said, "I'd be careful. I gave you stitches, but I'm not a professional. I don't know if they'll hold."

Johnny said, "How far out of Dillon are we?"

"Don't rightly know," she said. "We haven't actually been there. But we were told it's about twenty miles away."

"Long way for either of you to ride for a doctor."

She nodded.

Eli said, "I could do it. I'm almost a man, now."

Johnny nodded and couldn't help but smile.

He said, "Do you have parents?"

Eli said, "They died. Hers and mine both. We were on our way out here in a small wagon train, and they died."

Melissa Jean said, sort of shouting with a hushed voice, "Eli!"

"Sorry."

"Well," Johnny said to the boy. "Your name must be Eli."

The boy nodded.

"And you..," he looked at the girl.

Eli said, "Her name's Missy."

"Melissa Jean," the girl said, a little indignantly. She held out her hand. "Pleased to make your acquaintance."

Johnny shook her hand.

"Well, Melissa Jean, if you don't mind, I think I'm going to just stay here and rest a bit more before I try to stand up."

"I think that'd be wise."

Eli went outside to get an armful of wood. Keeping the wood box full was one of his chores around here. Melissa Jean came out with him.

Eli said, "Do you think he's one of 'em that's trying to find us?"

She shook her head. "I don't know. I hope Mister Jones gets back here soon."

The tracks Brown was following turned off of the trail. He followed them through a grove of pines, then up a rocky stretch.

He stood by his earlier gut feeling that the rider had to be Johnny McCabe, and McCabe was heading somewhere in particular. He hoped it would be the cabin of Jeb Jones. It would make his life easier.

He found throughout the world, men of similar walks-of-life tended to make each other's acquaintance, at one time or another. Jones had been a fur trapper in the days of old, and a scout for wagon trains in the forties and fifties. He had been known as an Indian fighter, and at times had lived among them. He had scouted for the Army and was known as a crack shot with a rifle. The kind of man a man like McCabe would probably be friends with.

Oh, it would be too easy, he thought, if McCabe led him right to Jeb Jones. But then, to do what Brown had to do, he might have to confront McCabe. He wasn't being paid enough for that.

Jones was old now, probably nearly eighty if the hear-say was true. He wouldn't be a problem to take down. Though, in his prime, he was another man Brown would demand a huge salary to confront.

He followed as the tracks moved in a northern direction. Then they seemed to stop and then start toward the southwest. As though the horse was wandering.

McCabe had to be injured, Brown figured. He had seen where McCabe had landed in the mud, and the dark spot was made by blood. Could he just be hanging onto the saddle while his horse wandered?

Brown found the tracks led him down a rocky slope toward a stream. It looked like the horse drank a little, and then it did something that perplexed him. It stepped into the water, and didn't step out.

An old trick, Brown knew. A way to hide your trail. A horse wouldn't do this on its own, so he figured McCabe must have been awake and turned the horse into the stream.

The question was, why would McCabe do this? Did he think he was being followed? Or did he just not want to leave a definable trail toward the cabin of Jeb Jones? Like old mountain men Brown had met, Jones was probably reclusive. Didn't want an easily discernable trail that led to his back door.

Brown knew his next step would be to ride along the stream and find the place where McCabe left the water. The problem was, there was no way to know which direction McCabe took.

Brown wanted those kids, but he was not going to face Johnny McCabe alone. He sure wasn't going to face McCabe and Jeb Jones together. He wasn't being paid nearly enough.

He decided to return to Dillon. The town had a telegraph station, and he intended to send a wire to his employers. If he was going to face McCabe, then they were going to have to pony-up some more money. Maybe enough so he could hire some men to ride with him. Such men were usually easy to find. Then he would be back, and he would find the trail left by McCabe's stallion and see if it could lead them to the cabin of Jeb Jones.

36

Johnny was feeling a little better, so he went out and grabbed an armful of wood for the stove.

It was late afternoon and a light rain had started falling. It was going to be above freezing tonight, but not by much.

He brought in a couple of armloads, then he decided that was enough. His head was starting to hurt and he felt a little unsteady. But he wanted to go out and see Thunder.

His stallion was waiting for him in a corral out back. One rail had fallen, and the other rails were low enough that Thunder could probably have jumped out if he wanted to.

Johnny walked up to the fence and Thunder came over.

Johnny reached and slapped a hand lightly to the horse's neck. The horse would accept a nose-rub only from Bree, though Johnny figured Melissa Jean could probably get away with it. Something about her energy, and the fact that Thunder had allowed her to strip off the saddle and put him in the corral.

Thunder made a whickering sound, and Johnny said, "I'm all right, old friend. It looks like I owe you my life."

It was near dark, and the rain had let up a little, but a misty fog was descending on them.

Johnny said, "Are you gonna be all right out here? I have to go in and lay down for a while. In a couple of days, when I'm feeling better, we'll skip that cattle auction and head home."

Johnny went back to the cabin. It was dark enough now that one window was lighted. Rain was starting to fall again.

Johnny stepped onto the porch, and that was when he heard the hammer of a gun being hauled back from behind him.

A man spoke, in an old crusty voice. "Don't you move nary a whisker, or I'll send you to kingdom-come."

Johnny could have kicked himself for letting a man get the draw on him. He tried to always be ready. Always watching. It was nothing he tried to do consciously, but was just usually aware. But the head wound had left him exhausted and unfocused.

"What're you doin' here?" the man said. "This is my cabin."

"It's a long story," Johnny said. "If I can turn around without you shooting me, I'll tell it."

The cabin door opened, and Melissa Jean stepped into the doorway.

"Mister Jones," she said. "I don't think he means us any trouble."

"What's your name?" the old man said. "And who sent you?"

Johnny looked over his shoulder at the man. His face was deeply lined, and he had white hair that fell to his shoulders, and a white beard. He wore a buckskin jacket and had a gray hat with a wide, floppy brim. In his hands was a buffalo rifle. Looked like a Sharps.

"My name is Johnny McCabe," Johnny said. "And no one sends me anywhere."

The old man was squinting. The sun was low in the sky, and the cabin and the land around was in shadows. But Johnny had noticed that old men who had lived most of their lives outdoors tended to squint by habit.

The old man's squint turned into a scowl of surprise. He said, "Johnny McCabe? The gunfighter?"

Johnny gave a sigh of resignation, and nodded his head. "Among other things. And it's occurring to me who you must be. Jeb Jones."

"What of it?"

"I've heard the name spoken a few times, that's all. Scout, fur trapper, Indian fighter."

The old man nodded. "Been all of that, and more."

He lowered his rifle. "Looks like you got some troubles."

Johnny nodded. "A bullet grazed my head. My horse brought me here."

Melissa Jean said, "He's telling the truth, Mister Jones."

Jones nodded. "Let's go inside and talk about it. You look like you're about to fall over."

Johnny had to admit, he could tolerate sitting down.

Jones called out to Eli. "My horse is in the trees back yonder. Go fetch it."

Eli said, "Yes, sir."

He slapped Eli on the shoulder. "We got us a whole load of deer meat to smoke."

Once they were inside, Johnny took a chair at the table. "Could use me some coffee," Jones said.

Johnny nodded. "Me too."

"Got me a can of it somewhere around here."

Melissa Jean went to a shelf and grabbed a can of Arbuckle's. She said, "I'll get some water heating."

Jones lowered himself into a chair across the table from Johnny. One knee snapped the way knuckles will.

He said, "I'm getting' too old to go traipsin' about the mountains."

He leaned his rifle against the table.

Johnny said, "I've got a rifle like that in my saddle."

"Used to use a Hawken. But it was gettin' old, so I replaced it with this 'un."

Johnny grinned. "We think alike. I have a Hawken standing in my rifle rack, back at the ranch."

Melissa Jean had a fire going in the stove, and she filled a kettle with water.

Jones said, "It's nice havin' a woman around the house. Don't know how I did it all alone, for so many years."

Johnny said, "She kin of yours?"

"No. Wish she was. She's like a daughter to me. And Eli's like a son."

Johnny nodded.

Jones said, "That don't surprise you none? That an old white man would consider a colored boy to be like a son?"

Johnny said, "One thing I've learned in my years is that the color of a man's skin means nothing. It's his backbone that counts. And his honor."

"We do think alike."

While they waited for the coffee, Johnny told Jeb about the cattle auction he had been going to.

Jeb said, "You see who shot you?"

Johnny shook his head. "I don't remember anything after I rode out of the town of Dillon."

"I come across a man on the ground, about ten miles back. Looks like a horse trampled him. Tracks on the ground, they tell a story. I figure that man shot you, then a horse kilt him. Prob'ly yours."

"How do you figure that?"

"Your horse has a loose shoe. Prob'ly got it loosened when he was driving it into that man's skull. I followed your tracks about as far as I could. They ended at a stream. I noticed somethin' else, too."

"What's that?"

"You were followed. There's a second set of tracks, a little fresher'n yours. A man followed you to the stream. That was when I give up tryin' to follow you, and headed right home."

Johnny's head was a little foggy, but his gut told him there was more to what was going on than he had been told.

He said, "If you don't mind my asking, what's going on here?"

"I might as well tell you. Your reputation as a good man has spread far and wide."

Johnny shrugged. "I don't know how good I am."

"Jim Austin said he met you once."

Johnny nodded. "Down Cheyenne way, maybe ten

years ago."

"He and I go way back. And he says his gut feelin' is you're a good man. So I'm gonna tell you. There's men out there what want these two young'uns dead."

Johnny blinked with surprise. "Dead?"

Melissa Jean said, "Yes sir, Mister McCabe."

"Why on Earth would anyone want to bring harm to you?"

"'Cause of what we know. And because of what we saw."

"And what did you see?"

"We saw the men who killed our parents."

37

Johnny's head wound was starting to smart, and he knew what it was. Infection setting in. And he knew what had to be done.

He said to Jeb, "There's a flask of corn squeezings in my saddle bags. I need to wash the wound out with that."

Jeb gave a squinting blink of surprise. "Why would you want to do that?"

Johnny told him the story. How he had learned from his old Texas Ranger captain that alcohol that's strong enough has a way of preventing infection.

After the wound was washed out, Johnny slept. Pain like that can take a lot out of a man.

When he awoke, the windows of the cabin were dark. Moonlight was drifting in, but it wasn't bright. Two nights before the storm, the last time Johnny had seen a clear night sky of late, the moon had been a smidge less than half.

In the moonlight, he could see Melissa Jean on the floor, with a pillow under her head and blankets pulled up to her chin.

He climbed out of the bunk and found Eli in the top bunk.

He decided he wanted to walk around a bit. Maybe go out and get some air.

He had left his gunbelt on the floor, so he could reach it from the bunk. He buckled it back on, then pushed his feet into his boots.

He stepped outside, finding the night air chilly. He liked this kind of night. Cool mountain air is good for cleaning out the lungs, he thought, and for cleaning out the soul.

Jeb Jones was seated on a bench in front of the cabin. He had a pipe in one hand and his rifle across his knees.

"Don't you sleep?" Johnny said.

Jeb shook his head. "Maybe come mornin'.""

"That rider who was trailing me has got you spooked."

Jeb nodded. "I don't want any harm to come to these young'uns. I love 'em like they were my own."

Johnny said, "I figure if I'm going to help you defend those two, I'd better have my rifle."

He fetched his Sharps from his saddle.

There was a chopping block a short ways from the cabin, so Johnny slid it over and used it as a stool to sit on.

He said, "Tell me about Melissa Jean and Eli."

Jeb took a puff of smoke from his pipe.

He said, "Their story begins in Alabama. Their daddy owned a plantation, back in the days of slavery. But he was one of them southern men you don't hear much about. The ones who didn't approve of slavery. He inherited the place when his father died, and one of the first things he did was free the slaves. Most of 'em stayed on. He couldn't afford to pay 'em a wage, but they had housing and meals, and he split the cotton and sugar cane crops with them."

"You say this like you know him."

Jeb nodded. "I was in St. Louis. He and his family were headin' west, along with Eli's family and a few others. There were only a few wagons. The days of the big wagon trains is long gone, and it's been a few years since I had worked as a guide for them. But they seemed like good folks, so I let them hire me."

Jeb told a story of Horatio Pike, whose mother was from Boston, and who had spent much time there with relatives when he was growing up, and adopted their views on abolition. After Pike inherited the plantation in Alabama, he freed his slaves and made them business partners. He and one of the former slaves, a man by the name of Otis Jackson, became friends.

"Melissa Jean is Pike's daughter. Their only child.

Otis Jackson and his wife had only one child, too."

Johnny said, "Eli."

Jeb nodded his head. "Melissa Jean and Eli were raised as practically brother and sister."

Jeb took another draw on his pipe, and continued his story. "All was lost when the northern soldiers arrived. They were tryin' to liberate the slaves. But on plantations like Pike's, where the colored folks weren't slaves, the soldiers drove 'em off anyway and burned the buildings. That happened more than you might think."

Johnny nodded. Granny Tate had told him her story.

Jeb said, "Pike and Jackson and a few others tried to rebuild, but their entire cotton crop and sugar crops were lost. They stayed on a few years, but the economy in the South was bad for a long time. It was in those years that Eli and Melissa Jean were born. Finally, both families decided to cash it in and head west."

"And that was when you met them."

Jeb nodded. "Brought 'em West. We only got so far, though, before the people who are after the kids caught up with 'em."

"What happened?"

"Kilt 'em all. Except for the youn'uns and me. And we barely got away with our lives."

38

Melissa Jean couldn't sleep. She had been lying on the pillow with her eyes shut, and heard Mr. McCabe strapping on his gun and stepping into his boots, and she heard the door as we went outside.

She remained in her blankets for a while and hoped sleep would catch her, but it didn't seem to want to.

Maybe it was because she was scared. She had heard Mr. Jones saying that Mr. McCabe had been followed. Mr. McCabe's horse had walked part of the way in a stream, and the man following him had given up and turned back. But the people who had killed Mama and Papa, and Eli's parents, were still out there.

Will they never leave us alone? She wondered.

She could hear the voices of Mr. Jones and Mr. McCabe. They were outside.

"Leave that door ajar," Mr. Jones said. "I always leave it that way when I'm outside, unless it's really could out. I want to be able to go in our out without the door hinge squeaking too much."

Mr. Jones chuckled and said, "Maybe I got that way from dealing with too many outlaws and hostile Indians over the years."

Mr. McCabe said, "I don't grease the hinges at my house, either, for pretty much the same reason."

Melissa Jean climbed out of the blankets and went barefoot to the door. From there, she could hear what they were talking about. Mr. Jones was telling about Melissa Jean and Eli. Telling Mr. McCabe their story.

*　　　*　　　*

Two Years Ago

Papa was not a tall man, but he stood straight and strong. He had dark hair and an impressive, thick mustache. He was standing in front of the ruins of the big mansion he and Mama had once lived in.

Further back were the former slave quarters. Cabins that consisted of two or three rooms. Each cabin had a chimney and a fireplace, and a floor made of wooden floorboards. Many plantations had slave quarters with dirt floors, but Papa had always said all people are equal in the eyes of the Lord, so he made sure the people working for him had decent quarters.

Papa was talking to Aunt Agatha. She and Uncle Wilbert were visiting from Boston. Aunt Agatha had a long nose and a perpetual scowl that Melissa Jean thought were unfortunate, until she got to know the woman a little. Now she thought the nose and the scowl were fitting.

"Horatio," she said, "I don't see why you live like this. Why don't you rebuild?"

She was referring to the ruins of the mansion. Two walls were still standing, but blackened by the fire the Yankee soldiers had started when they burned the place. The roof had burned and then fell in. A stone chimney, standing tall and proud, the only reminder of the life the family had enjoyed before the War. A life Melissa Jean had only heard about. She had been born three years after the war ended. The only home she had really known was the small farmhouse Papa had built for them after the mansion was lost.

Papa said to the scowly old woman, "There's no money left, Aunt Agatha."

"I can't believe that. *Acadia* was one of the finest plantations in Virginia. I can't believe the money is all gone."

"Our funds were frozen by the government during the War. What little we had in paper money was lost when the house was burned."

Melissa Jean was watching from a wooden swing that was suspended by ropes from a low branch of an old oak tree. She still thought of herself as Missy, in those days. She was in a checkered dress, and her light-colored hair was tied into two long braids.

She wasn't supposed to be listening. Papa and Aunt Agatha were talking grown-up stuff. Mama always said when grownups were talking grown-up business, children shouldn't eavesdrop.

However, Missy was about to turn thirteen. Not much younger than marrying age in some of the more remote areas, so she didn't feel too guilty about listening.

Aunt Agatha was giving Papa a long look. It was exaggerated by that long, hooked nose of hers.

Finally she said, "Horatio, I knew my brother well. He began this plantation, and he built it into one of the best, brightest, most profitable plantations in the South. I find it hard to believe that all of that money is simply gone."

He shrugged. "Well, it is, Aunt Agatha."

She gave a *hmmph* sound, and looked away.

That afternoon, she and Uncle Wilbert were on a stagecoach headed for Birmingham. From there, they would be catching a train that would eventually get them back to Boston.

Good place for them, Missy thought. *As far from here as possible.*

As Papa left, taking them in a carriage to town, Eli walked over to Missy. He was in overalls and he wore no shoes. He and Missy were often barefoot most of the summer.

He said, "Just who was that mean old woman?"

"Papa's Aunt Agatha. His great Aunt, really."

"I don't see a whole lot great about her."

Missy smiled. "Me neither. It was her brother, Uncle Mordecai, who was Papa's father. My grandfather. Left this whole place to Papa."

That night, in the small farmhouse Papa had built, Papa and Mama sat at the kitchen table having one last cup of coffee before turning in. It was late, and Missy was upstairs and long asleep. Or so they thought. She was actually at the head of the stairs listening. Even then, she found out a lot of stuff by listening when people didn't realize she was there.

Once, Eli had criticized her for it. He said, "Missy, you shouldn't do that. Ma calls it *eavesdroppin'*."

"Papa told me you've got to learn about how the world works if you hope to survive in it. He also said the best way to learn is to keep your mouth shut and listen. So that's what I'm doing. I'm listening."

And so she listened, from the top of the stairs.

Mama said, "What do you think that old woman wants? Do you really think she believes we have some money stashed away?"

"She seems to think so. I don't know why. It's true my father was quite wealthy and left much of it to us, including this place. If we had access to all of the funds we had before the War, we could have rebuilt the main house, and we could have built better housing for the few people who are still here working for us. Acadia was once a grand plantation, but now it's really just a poor, cotton farm. Nothing left of the sugar crop at all."

"What do you think she wants?"

"I think she's mad that Mordecai left the whole thing to us and not her. She wants us to give her some of the money, but can't accept that the money's now no longer there."

There was a pause. Missy figured Mama was taking a sip of coffee.

Mama said, "Well, I hope she never comes back."

Papa said, with a sort of grim, defeated tone, "I have a feeling we haven't heard the last of her."

*   *   *

It was late September when Missy learned some more stuff from the top of the stairs. It was evening, and she had been sent to bed. Eli was upstairs, too, in the extra bedroom that served as a guest room. His mother and father were downstairs with Mama and Papa, talking about the year's cotton crop.

Missy didn't know much about business, and she had no part in growing cotton. But she knew it had been bad. A long dry spell, to start with. Papa told her you need a lot of water for cotton to grow. Then came problems with boll weevils. The little buggers were the bane of cotton farmers everywhere, but this year they were especially bad. Then an early frost was the final nail in the coffin.

She heard Papa say, "I was hanging on, hoping we could salvage at least half the crop. But it was that frost last week that really did us in."

They were in the parlor, down at the foot of the stairs.

"How much do you think we can take from it?" Harley Jackson said.

"I don't know. Not even twenty percent, I don't think."

Eli was suddenly at Missy's side. The boy could sure walk quiet.

"What are you doing up?" Missy whispered.

"I came out here to learn stuff, like you."

"Well, keep it quiet."

Downstairs, Mama was saying, "How are we going to pay our debts? Will they foreclose on us?"

"I don't know, Mary," Papa said.

For the first time in her life, Missy was really scared. She had been scared of little kid stuff before. Afraid there was a monster under the bed, and Papa had to hold a lamp down low while she peeked under so she could be reassured there was nothing there. But she had never been afraid of losing her home. She had never even thought about it before. She realized this was the kind of thing grownups feared, the kind of thing that kept them up at night.

There was more talk on other evenings, and Missy and Eli listened then, too. It was during these talks that

Mama and Papa and Eli's parents decided to let the farm go, and to pack up and head west.

*   *   *

One Year Ago

There were four wagons. The Pikes had one, the Jacksons had another, and they had joined with two other families. They had pooled their money together and hired Jeb Jones to guide them west. Mr. Jones had been a scout back in the old days, before Missy and Eli were born. Back then, wagon trains sometimes stretched a mile long, making their way to Oregon or the gold fields in California.

It was when they were in Nebraska that the trouble started.

Eli was on the back of a small horse they had brought with them. The horse reared up and Eli slid off the back and landed in the grass. Missy came running.

He wasn't hurt, but the horse galloped off.

Eli got to his feet and said, "I'll get it."

He took off running, with Missy right behind.

Mama called out from the wagon, "Missy! Eli! Don't go far!"

Missy and Eli followed the horse, cutting their way through an ocean of grass that was knee-high. The land all around them was open and wide, with grass that grew to the horizon. The wind would blow the grass in ripples like ocean waves. Missy had never seen the like.

But the horse didn't want to be caught. He would stand, munching on the grass, until Eli and Missy got to within reaching distance, and then he would turn and run off. He covered a quarter mile one time and then stopped, and they had to trudge after him.

Missy wasn't keeping track of the distance. Neither was Eli. They had been gone at least an hour, maybe more—neither one of them had a pocket watch.

Mr. Jones could tell the time by the position of the sun, but Missy didn't know how to do that.

Finally, Eli got his hands on the reins and said, "Got-cha."

But then Missy and Eli looked around and realized the wagons weren't in sight. Just the long, stretched-out grasslands.

"Eli," she said, "I think we're lost."

"No we ain't," he said. "All we gotta do is follow our path back, where we cut through the grass."

There was indeed a small line through the grass behind them, where they had passed through. But the wind was blowing, and the grass was rippling and waving. They hadn't been backtracking more than ten minutes when they found their trail through the grass was disappearing. Soon it was gone entirely.

"What do we do now?" she said.

"The trail has to be south of here."

"How do you know?"

"Because we were north of the wagon trail when we started out, and we ain't crossed over the trail, have we?"

She shook her head. Made sense. But she had to admit she was scared.

"Where's south?" she said.

He had to stop and think about that.

"Sun rises in the east," he said. "Sets in the west."

The sun was drifting downward toward one horizon. Missy said, "Then that must be west."

He nodded.

"So," she said. "Where's south?"

Figuring this out was harder than it looked, she realized. But Eli wouldn't admit it.

"Ever seen a compass?" he said.

She nodded.

"Okay. So if this is west," he held one arm toward the sun, "then this has to be east," he held his other arm in the other direction.

Missy said, "So, then where would south be?"

That was when they saw a rider coming toward them. It was Mr. Jones.

Missy felt the fear fall away. "Mister Jones!" she called out.

He was old, but he rode a horse like he was born to it. When Eli rode, his butt tended to bounce in the saddle, but Mr. Jones rode like he was somehow connected to the horse. Like they were one being.

He reined up. "Your parents sent me lookin' for you two," he said. "Come on, let's go."

Mr. Jones reached down with one hand and took Missy's hand and pulled her up and onto the back of the horse behind him. Eli climbed into the saddle of the horse he and Missy had tried so hard to catch.

They rode a while—Missy had no idea how far. It seemed like a long way. There was a low grassy hill ahead of them, and a small stand of trees to one side. She didn't know what kind they were.

Mr. Jones said, "The wagons are just beyond that hill."

That was when they heard the gunfire. Lots of it.

"What's that?" she said.

Eli tried to kick his horse into a gallop, but Mr. Jones reached out and grabbed the rein.

Missy didn't know a lot about guns, but she knew the pistol Papa carried made a different sound than the big rifle Mr. Jones had in his saddle. She thought there might have been three or four guns going off.

Mr. Jones made them wait until the shooting stopped. Then he told them to hide behind those trees while he took a look.

Missy and Eli watched from hiding while Mr. Jones rode to nearly the top of the hill. Then he pulled his rifle and swung out of the saddle and got down on all fours, and he crawled through the grass to the top of the hill. He was there a while.

When he finally came back, he pulled Missy onto the horse behind him again and told Eli to mount up.

"What happened?" Missy said.

Mr. Jones didn't answer but started riding.

He didn't head toward the hill. Instead, he took them away, in the opposite direction.

That night, they made what Mr. Jones called dry camp in a small grassy gulch. He said he didn't want a fire because the flames could be visible from a distance.

They chewed on jerked venison from his saddle bags, and then Missy and Eli sat in the grass with Mr. Jones' blankets wrapped around them. He sat beside them, his rifle across his lap.

It was then that he told them what he had seen. Three men had attacked the wagons. Shot and killed everyone there.

Missy would have cried, but she had already figured something bad had happened. And out here in the Nebraska night, with miles of open grassland all around them and some apparently dangerous men out there, the need to cry seemed to be pushed aside by the need to survive.

While Mr. Jones had been watching, hidden in the grass at the top of the hill, the men began unloading the wagons. Then they began to open crates and bags.

He said, "It was like they were lookin' for somethin'."

"It was that old lady," Eli said. "The one with the long nose and the scary face. Had to be. Lookin' for that money she thinks your Papa has."

Missy wanted to call him wrong. To say it was a silly notion. But was it?

*   *   *

They rode for a few days and stopped at a collection of buildings. Mr. Jones called it Fort Laramie, but it didn't look like what Missy thought a fort would look like. Just buildings scattered around. There was no wall at all.

It was night when they rode in, and Mr. Jones left Missy and Eli standing in a doorway while he went to buy some supplies.

"Don't move none," he said. "I won't be long."

So they stood where they were. The building was dark. Looked to be some sort of restaurant, but it was nearly midnight and the place was closed.

They were standing and waiting when a man walked up. Missy couldn't see his face because it was lost in shadows. The only light was from the moon overhead, and his hat had a wide brim that shaded his entire face. But he wore a gun at his right side and a long knife at his left.

"You the Pike girl?" he said.

Missy didn't dare say anything.

"Must be," he said. "They said you were travelin' with a darkie boy."

Missy was truly scared. She said nothing and neither did Eli.

"You're gonna tell me where the money is," he said. "We know your pappy had some, from that plantation. I was hired to find out where he hid it and then stick a knife in you both. But if you tell me, I'll let you live."

"There ain't no money," Eli said.

"Then in that case, you're both gonna die."

That was when Mr. Jones stepped up behind him with, his knife out. He tapped the man on the shoulder and when the man turned, Mr. Jones drove his knife into the man, all the way to the hilt.

Missy gasped and stood staring.

Mr. Jones then pulled the knife out and the man felt to his knees, and then went down face-forward.

Mr. Jones said, "Come on. Let's get out of here."

She had never seen anything like this in her life. But her feet somehow moved, like they had a will of their own. She followed Mr. Jones and Eli to the horses, and they rode on out into the night.

"It ain't safe," Mr. Jones said. "They're not gonna stop lookin' for you."

"There's no money," Missy said. "None at all."

"Don't matter none. What matters is they think there's some. Apparently, they think there's a lot. They won't stop tryin' to find you."

"What'll we do?"

"I got me a cabin, off in the mountains in Idaho Territory. It's a fair ride from here, but they shouldn't find you there."

*   *

*

And yet they had, she thought, as she stood in the doorway listening to Mr. Jones tell Mr. McCabe all about it.

Mr. Jones had brought her and Eli to this cabin nearly a year ago. She now liked to be called *Melissa Jean*, though no one seemed to call her that. Except for Mr. McCabe. Eli insisted on calling her *Missy*, just because it bugged her. He was good at being a bratty younger brother. Mr. Jones always called her *young lady* or *ma'am*.

"I know one thing," Mr. McCabe said. "I'm with you. I'm not going to let anything happen to those children."

Suddenly, just hearing him say those words, she felt like a heavy weight was lifted from her shoulders. There was something about Mr. McCabe, a certain power he seemed to have. Like he wasn't afraid of anything. When he said those words, she felt like maybe she and Eli were really safe.

She crawled back into her blankets and fell fast asleep.

39

Brown sent a telegram to Denver. *I might have to face Johnny McCabe. I want triple pay and money to hire some men.* Of course, as with any telegram, it was sent not with a period between sentences, as there was no Morse Code for a period, so he used the word *stop*.

He was heading to the lounge in the Corinne for a drink and told the telegrapher to deliver the response to him there.

He ordered a glass of red wine and took a corner table. As always, with his back to the wall.

There were four men at the bar. They looked like drifters, but they wore their guns like they knew how to use them. Positioned for easy access. One man had a bandolier draped across his chest. Marshal Brantley was talking to them. Brown supposed Brantley was trying to make sure they weren't looking for trouble.

Brown watched while he sipped his wine. It occurred to him that he would go down in history as the man who killed Johnny McCabe.

The American frontier was a place that was quickly producing heroes. Men who for some reason were viewed in a larger-than-life way. Becoming the proverbial legends in their own time. Few stood on the level of Johnny McCabe, and the man who killed him would be famous in his own right.

However, Brown didn't need that kind of fame. In his business, it was best to retain anonymity. The name of Theodore Brown might go down in history, but he would also be known as a man who would disappear from the historical record shortly afterward. Brown intended to discard the name and not use it again.

Brantley finished with the men and left the barroom. Apparently satisfied that they were going to leave town and cause no trouble.

Brown took another sip of wine, and a boy working for the telegrapher arrived with a response. A boy in his mid-teens, Brown figured. Thin, a mop of hair, and the uncertain look of a boy who wanted to be a man but wasn't quite there yet.

He gave Brown an envelope and Brown flipped him a dime. Then he opened the envelope and read the telegram. His employers were all too eager to triple his salary and include more money so he could hire some men. The money was being wired to him at a local bank in Dillon.

Whatever money that was hidden, the whereabouts known only by those children, Brown figured it must be an obscene amount. It occurred to him that once he learned the location of the money, it would be all too easy to simply run out on his contract and take the money himself.

He got to his feet, holding his glass of wine in one hand. He held it in his left so his right could be free should he need to draw his gun. McCabe wasn't the only one who went through life in a constant state of readiness.

He might need more than four men, but these four would be a good starting point. He walked over to them and said, "Boys, how would you like a job?"

40

The eastern sky was alight with morning, but the sun wasn't quite in view, yet. Morning birds were singing and the air was rich with earthen smells and the scent of pine.

Jeb Jones stood in front of his cabin with a tin cup filled with coffee. He had a Colt .44 tucked into the front of his belt, and he leaned his rifle against a tree stump.

He looked back at his cabin and shook his head. "This old cabin has been here a lot of years. It's seen better times."

Johnny McCabe was standing beside him, a cup of coffee in one hand. He said, "You build it?"

Jeb shook his head. "Found it, about twenty years ago. Must've been built by a trapper. I found the remains of a man, about a half mile away, at the bottom of a slope. I figure he had died a few years before. Not much of the body left, just bones. One leg was busted just above the knee. I figger he was out tending to his traps and fell down the slope. Maybe got caught in a small snow slide. It can happen if you ain't careful."

Johnny nodded his head. He knew these mountains and what they were capable of.

Jeb said, "I made new shingles for the roof. Made door new hinges out of leather. The door was hanging loose when I first found the place. Put new mud in between the stones of the chimney. I done more repairs on it over the years. There's some gaps between the logs now, that need to be filled in when I can get to it.

"It's good to have a place to come back to, if you need to. Never figured on having to defend against an attack, though. Ain't fortified all that well. The strength of the place is that it's hidden so well. You wouldn't know it was here unless you rode up onto it. I burn the driest wood I can find, so there's little smoke."

Johnny decided he needed to sit down. He moved the rifle aside and sat on the stump.

"Still a little shaky," he said. "I get dizzy sometimes."

"It's that head wound. You got a concussion."

"I figure so."

"I noticed when you was cleanin' that wound out with your corn squeezin's, if your hair goes the right way, there's a scar you can see above your right ear. You been shot like that before."

Johnny nodded. "Years ago, back in Pennsylvania. The man who shot my father shot at me, too. The bullet grazed my head. I've been shot a few times. Most recently, four summers ago. Took two bullets that time. The lead's still in me. I still feel it sometimes."

"You live the lives we do, you tend to get scars. I got more'n my share of 'em."

Jeb took a sip of coffee. "Listen, McCabe, I've been thinkin'. These young'uns, they've been with me a year, now. They've become like my own. I'd hate for something to happen to them. But I'm old. Ain't gonna be around forever. You seem like a good man, and I ain't normally one to ask favors or to ask them lightly."

"What do you need?"

"I want you to look after 'em, if anything happens to me. See that they're taken care of."

Johnny nodded. "You have my word."

Johnny looked at the cabin. He agreed, it wasn't well fortified. The trees that helped conceal the place could also give an attacker cover.

"You know," he said, "we may not have to defend this place, after all."

"What're you thinkin'?"

"I got a ranch a two day ride northeast of Dillon. No one will take those children from that ranch. I've got enough men who are good with their guns, and a lot of friends I can call on. That place is well-fortified. I built it that way."

"A two day ride can be a long ways, in your

condition. I don't think you could last a half hour in the saddle."

Johnny nodded. "We just have to wait it out. A few more days, and I might be ready to ride."

"In the meantime, once this coffee is done, I think I might saddle up and take a ride around these hills and cut for sign. See if anyone has been pokin' around."

"Be careful out there. If anyone sees you, they can follow you right to this cabin, and I'm in no shape for a gun battle."

Jeb grinned. "Ain't a man alive can see me, if'n I don't want to be seen."

Johnny couldn't help but return the grin. "Have you ever met my brother Joe? The Cheyenne call him *Nakhoe*. Means *bear*."

"A grizzly of man. I met him once. Years ago."

"Somehow, I'm not surprised."

41

Johnny McCabe stood in front of the cabin. He had removed the makeshift bandage that Melissa Jean had fixed for him. He wanted to let some air get to the wound. Jeb had a small, broken shard of mirror held to a cabin wall by a couple of nails. With it, Johnny could see the wound looked like it was healing well. The most important thing was there was no infection.

He wanted to do some target practice, to see how steady his hand was, but he didn't dare. A gunshot could be heard from a distance, so he thought he would try at least drawing the gun. He pulled the gun and brought his gun hand out to full extension. One smooth, quick motion. It didn't feel right, though. His hand felt a little shaky. He slid the gun back into his holster and drew again. It felt a little better. But when he tried it a third time, his hand missed the gun altogether.

He remembered years ago, Zack Johnson had been thrown by a horse and hit his head. Granny Tate said it was a bad concussion. She said he might not be right for two or three weeks. It had now been five days since Johnny had been shot. Full recovery might take a while.

Behind him, Eli was splitting wood. The boy stood almost to Johnny's shoulder. Not big, but he was strong. Eli brought the axe down and with one strike, and a chunk of wood split apart into two smaller pieces.

Johnny walked over. "You handle that axe well."

Eli nodded. "Been splittin' wood ever since I was old enough to lift an axe. Can use a hammer and a saw too. Can ride a horse. I can even do smithy work."

"You ever shoot a gun?"

He nodded again. "Mister Jones, he been showin' me how to shoot."

"You've been through a lot, this past year. You and Melissa Jean."

"Yessir. Our parents are dead. Our home is gone. All we got is each other, and Mister Jones and this cabin."

Johnny had been through a lot in his life, but at Eli's age, he had been safe in his home, back on the family farm in Pennsylvania.

Johnny said, "What's your full name, Eli?"

"Elijah Jackson. But Jackson ain't our real name."

"What is?"

He shrugged. "Don't rightly know. Ain't got one, I guess. Jackson is just a slave name. My mother and father were owned by Mordecai Jackson, Missy's grandfather. We got his name. When Missy's father freed us, we kept the name. Didn't know any other name to take."

Eli went back to working on the wood pile. Johnny stood watching, and he thought about what Eli had said. One man owning another. Not having a name. Eli looked like a boy with a lot of backbone, who was growing into a good man.

Seemed like he ought to have a name, Johnny thought. A real one.

It was nightfall when Jeb returned. Eli took his horse, stripped the saddle off and rubbed the horse down, while Jeb went into the cabin for a cup of coffee. Melissa Jean had just made a pot.

"Smelled the smoke of this fire from nearly a quarter mile away," he said. "That's too far."

Johnny was at the table, with his own cup of coffee. He said, "The nights in these mountains are still a little chilly. Going without a fire is going to be hard on Melissa Jean and Eli."

"I got extra blankets." Jeb leaned his rifle against the table, then poured a cup of coffee and sat.

He said, "I seen six riders. The closest they got was about two miles off. But they're workin' their way in this direction."

"Gunmen?"

Jeb nodded. "They're lookin' through every possible piece of land they can find. They're takin' their time, to make sure they don't miss a thing. Every gulch, every patch of woods. Every pass between ridges."

"Then, it's only a matter of time before they find us."

Jeb nodded. "Looks that way."

"Then, come morning, I suggest we saddle up and ride."

"You ain't recovered enough yet for a long ride."

"We're gonna have to go anyway."

42

The following morning, Johnny finished his coffee on the porch. He figured this was the last time he would see the little cabin.

He liked this area. A rocky cliff rose up not far from the cabin and Johnny had a good view of it as he stood with his coffee. The morning rays were giving the exposed rock an orange glow. Ponderosa pines stood tall around the cabin, and the air was clean. The old Shoshone shaman who had taught Johnny so much would have said this place was surrounded by good spirits.

There had been a time when Johnny would roam the mountains and seek out sections of land like this. Not when the children were younger, but once they were grown, he didn't feel as much need to be home. Jack was off at medical school in those days, Josh was turning into a fine cowhand, and Bree was becoming a young woman. Aunt Ginny was there, and Johnny felt he could allow himself time to simply roam the mountains. Experience the good spirits the old shaman spoke of.

And those had been the days when he was still burning inside because of the loss of Lura.

Now, he had Jessica to return to, and they had young children. Cora and the twins. Now Johnny had a need to be home, and there was no more burning inside. As nice as this little section of mountains was, as easy as this place was on his soul, he wanted to get home.

To make matters more pressing, Johnny was in no condition for a gun battle.

Jeb had gone out to the small barn earlier, and now he came riding up to the porch.

Johnny said, "As soon as this coffee is gone, I'm going to saddle Thunder and Eli's horse."

"I still don't think you're up to a full day in the saddle."

Johnny shrugged. "I don't see as though I have much choice."

Jeb nodded. Johnny knew Jeb was right, but Jeb saw that Johnny was right, too.

Jeb said, "Eli can help you with those horses. He can saddle a horse fine."

"Probably not Thunder. That stallion is half-wild. Won't let most people near him."

"And don't forget, your horse has a bad shoe. He may not be able to travel fast."

"Thunder will do what's needed. He always has."

Jeb said, "I'm gonna go and scout the area. If I'm not back, don't wait for me. I'll catch up with you."

He turned his horse away, and rode off through the pines.

That old man is tough as nails, Johnny thought. Not that different from old Ches, back at the ranch, or Mr. Chen in Jubilee. The difference being that Ches was a cowhand, and Jeb was a mountain man. And Chen was, well, Johnny had never really been sure.

Johnny hoped to be as tough and capable when he got to their age.

When his cup was empty, he decided it was time to start saddling the horses. Whether he was ready to ride or not.

That was when Jeb came galloping back, hanging onto his hat with one hand, his horse's mane flying wildly.

"They're comin'!" he called out. "We run out of time!"

43

Johnny ran into the cabin. Melissa Jean was at the stove, and Eli was stuffing supplies into saddle bags. Cans of beans, a sack of flour.

Johnny said, "They're here."

Melissa Jean looked at him, her eyes wide.

Johnny said, "Mister Jones and I won't let them take you."

She nodded, but she was still scared.

Johnny knew they didn't have much time. He said to Eli, "You said you can shoot."

Eli nodded. "Yes, sir."

Johnny went to his saddle bags and pulled out his two old-school Remington revolvers.

"I don't carry them anymore, but I always bring them with me. Just in case. Cartridges aren't all that reliable. They can misfire, sometimes. These guns don't take cartridges."

Eli nodded. "I know how they work. My daddy and Missy's had guns like them."

Johnny handed them to Eli, and Eli tucked one into his belt and held the other in his right hand.

Johnny said, "You have ten shots, between the two guns. Make them count."

Eli nodded.

Johnny said, "This is a hard thing to do, at your age. You might have to kill a man, today."

Eli said, "I'll be all right."

And Johnny realized, Eli would be. The boy didn't have fear in his eyes. He didn't have anger, either. He seemed calm. Like he was about to do what he had to do, and his spirit had somehow accepted it.

Johnny saw something of himself in the boy.

Jeb came running in, hobbling a little on his old knees.

He said, "They're here."

Johnny went to a window, drawing his gun. Six riders were reining up in front of the cabin.

Johnny had to make a shot, but he didn't know if he could do it with a pistol. His concussion was passing, a little more every day, but he still wasn't quite steady enough.

He said, "Melissa Jean, fetch me my rifle."

She did, handing it to him.

Then he said, "Get down on the floor. As flat as you can."

She did.

Eli took a window, and Jeb was with him.

Johnny said, "Eli, take the window over by the stove. If they come around back, let 'em know it was a mistake."

"Yessir," Eli said.

Johnny holstered his revolver and brought up his rifle.

"What do you have in mind?" Jeb said.

"To cut the head off the snake."

One of the men was calling out. "You in the cabin! We know you have those children in there."

A British accent, Johnny thought. Kind of strange. But he wasn't going to be allowed much time to think about it.

Johnny cocked the rifle and brought it to his shoulder. He had always taught his children not to cock a gun until you're aiming it. But somehow, over the years, he had developed the habit of cocking his rifle before he drew a bead on a target. He had done it with his old Hawken years ago. Something else he wasn't going to have much time to think about.

The man called out, "I know you're in there!"

Jeb called back, "Ride out now, and no one gets hurt!"

There was no glass in the cabin windows. Jeb used wooden shutters at night to keep the cold out.

Johnny drew a bead on the man with the accent. Despite what was left of the concussion, and that he noticed the sight on his rifle trembling a little, he felt the usual calmness overtaking him. The calmness that came before a gunfight. The same feeling that went along with the look Eli had in his eye a moment ago.

That was when Johnny realized he knew this man. The writer from back East, who had been at the Corinne a week ago. Johnny had thought back then that the man was no tenderfoot. He moved like a fighter. The man was now wearing a gun at his side and had a rifle in his hands. Not a Winchester or an older Spencer, like most men in the area carried. It was some sort of bolt-action rifle. European maybe. One more thing Johnny wasn't going to have much time to think about.

He let out a slow exhale, the same way you do when you're shooting an arrow, and he pulled the trigger. The gun bucked against his shoulder, and the man with the accent pitched back in the saddle and slid off the horse's rump onto the ground.

The men kicked their horses into action, wheeling around heading for the pines that grew within shooting distance of the house.

Johnny leaned his rifle against the wall. The rifle was a single-shot, and he wasn't going to take the time to reload it.

Johnny said to Jeb, "Always take out the leader first, if you can."

The gunmen began shooting at the cabin. Johnny and Jeb both ducked down. Bullets tore into the log walls, tearing away chips of wood. A bullet shot through the open window and hit the wall above the stove, and Eli ducked.

Johnny then raised his head to get a look outside. He saw a man's shoulder and arm from behind a tree, and he pointed his pistol and fired. The shot was a little off, hitting the tree but not the man, and the man ducked away.

Jeb had his pistol out and was firing. The gunmen were returning fire.

Johnny saw two cut off to one side.

Jeb said, "They're tryin' to get behind us."

Johnny said, "Eli, be ready."

Eli said, "I am."

Johnny thought, *Somehow I know you are.*

Johnny saw Eli raise a pistol and fire out a window.

Eli said, "Got him."

Then bullets started tearing into the back wall, and Eli was returning fire. Shots started again from out front, and Johnny and Jeb began returning fire as well.

Johnny's Colt was empty, so he flipped open the loading gate and began dumping out the empties and thumbing in new cartridges. One of Eli's guns was empty, so he tossed it aside and grabbed the second one.

One man out front stepped a bit away from the tree he was using for cover, and had a Winchester to his shoulder. Johnny raised his pistol. The man fired, and then Johnny pulled the trigger and the man went down.

"Mister Jones!" Melissa Jean screamed.

Johnny looked over at Jeb. The old man had fallen back and away from the window, and was sitting on the floor. The man with the rifle had got him.

"Jeb," Johnny said.

But Jeb didn't respond. He began to rise, like he was heading back to the window, but then his legs folded and he went down face first onto the floor. He rolled over, on his back.

Melissa Jean scrambled to him. "Mister Jones!"

She knelt at his side. "Don't die," she said. "Please don't die."

Jeb was gasping for air. Johnny could see it was a body shot. Maybe hit a lung. Johnny didn't think it looked good.

"Please don't die," Melissa Jean said again.

Jeb said, "Sometimes..," he sucked in some air, "we don't have much choice."

The men out front had realized the shooting had stopped, and they had heard Melissa Jean's scream.

They were stepping out from behind the trees and walking toward the house, holding their rifles ready.

Time for one of the stunts people will talk about later, Johnny thought. He had never been known for trick-shooting with his left, but that didn't mean he couldn't. It was just that he had seldom needed to.

He scrambled over to Jeb and Melissa Jean. Tears were streaming down her face like little rivers, and Jeb's eyes were open but Johnny didn't think he was seeing anything anymore.

Again, no time to think about it now. Johnny grabbed Jeb's pistol.

Johnny always counted the shots in a gunfight. Eli had two shots remaining, and there was one left in Jeb's gun.

Johnny took the gun in his left and his own pistol in his right, and cocked them both.

The men were about a hundred feet away now, advancing at a steady walk.

Johnny raised both pistols out the window, focusing on two targets at once, and pulled both triggers.

One man spun around, staggered a bit and then fell. The other one's knees buckled and he dropped, like a puppet with its strings cut.

The third man went sprinting off to his right as Johnny fired again. Johnny's shot missed, and the man dove for cover behind a tree stump.

"Oh, Mister Jones," Melissa Jean was saying.

That was when the dizziness hit Johnny. Like a sledgehammer falling on him. He dropped Jeb's pistol, and he placed his left hand flat against the wall to steady himself. He looked out the window to see if he could get a shot at the man by the stump, but all was blurry.

A gun was fired, and he ducked back.

He didn't think the gun was fired from the stump. Must have been one of the men he had shot. The man apparently wasn't quite dead.

Johnny had a feeling he had never had before. The feeling that this gunfight might be his last.

The man from out back had run around to the front of the cabin, and he kicked open the front door. He charged in, his pistol ready.

Eli spun and fired, and the man's body was jolted with the impact of the bullet. He looked at Eli and raised his gun for a shot, but Eli fired again. The man's gun went off, the bullet ringing against the stove. The man dropped to his knees and then sprawled face-down on the floor.

Johnny chanced a look out the window again. His vision was coming into full focus.

The first man Johnny had shot-the one he had recognized from Dillon--was on his feet, looking a little wobbly, but trying to run toward the cabin.

That was when Thunder came charging in from nowhere. He had been in the corral earlier, when Johnny was out front with his coffee. The horse must have jumped the railing.

The man turned at the sound of the horse bearing down on him, and the horse slammed him hard. The man landed on the ground with a bounce, and then the horse was on him.

The gunman behind the stump shot at Thunder, and Johnny fired at the man. Neither shot found its target.

Thunder was jumping on the man, tearing at him with his hooves.

The gunman fired again and Johnny saw a small flash of blood at Thunder's hip.

The horse turned and began running toward the pines. The man at the stump raised his gun for a shot, but Johnny fired at him. The bullet hit the stump and sent wood chips flying, and the man ducked back.

The dizziness rose a notch, and Johnny had to drop back to the floor, sitting with one shoulder against the wall.

Eli said, "Have you been hit?"

Johnny shook his head. "I'll be all right. Just give me a second."

Eli got to his feet and ran to the door.

Johnny said, "Eli..,"

Eli said, "There's only one left. He's mine."

Eli went out the door.

44

The dizziness was passing as quickly as it had come on, but Johnny felt unsteady. Weak. Like he needed a long nap.

He looked over at the body on the floor. The gunman Eli had shot. Both of the Remingtons were on the floor, but Johnny noticed the gun that had been in the man's hand was now missing.

Johnny looked out the window and saw Eli standing in full view. Eli's hands were in the air.

Eli said, "I surrender. Come on out. I'll tell you where the money is. Just don't hurt us."

The gunman rose from behind the stump. "Where's the girl, you little darkie?"

Eli said, "In the house, sir."

"We been paid a lot of money to bring the both of you in. There's a woman down in Denver wants to have a word with both of you."

Eli nodded. He let his hands drift downward.

"Now you stay right there, or I'll send you to your maker," the man said.

Eli said, "Only if you can shoot me first."

That was when Johnny saw the revolver tucked into the back pocket of Eli's pants. He had taken the gun of the man who had charged into the cabin.

The man looked with disbelief in his eyes as Eli brought the gun around, cocking it as he moved. The man didn't even get his gun up before Eli fired.

The man took a staggering step, and he raised his gun and fired. The bullet burned the side of Eli's shoulder, and he dropped to one knee and fired again. The man went over backwards and landed in the dirt.

Eli cocked the gun again and waited, but the man wasn't moving anymore.

Eli then rose to his feet, released the hammer of the gun and looked back at the cabin. A trickle of blood was running down one arm. He nodded to Johnny, and Johnny nodded back.

Then Thunder came trotting over to Eli. The boy looked at a streak of red across Thunder's rump, and he said, "Looks like you and me both are the worse for wear. But we won. I wasn't gonna let anyone hurt Missy, and I guess you weren't either."

The horse shook his head and snorted, and then reared up, kicking its hooves into the air. Eli nodded and smiled.

Johnny came out of the cabin and walked up to them.

Thunder was now down on all fours, and Johnny gave him a couple of pats to the side of his neck. Johnny glanced at the streak of red on Thunder's rump, where the bullet had grazed him. It would be sore for a little while, but the horse would be all right.

Johnny then shifted his gaze to Eli's shoulder. The skin was torn a bit, like a bad cut, and a trickle of blood had reached his elbow. But, like Thunder, he would be all right.

"What that man called you was wrong," Johnny said. "What you are, is a gunhawk."

45

They buried Jeb Jones the following morning in front of the cabin. They situated the grave so Jeb would always be facing the rising sun.

Johnny found working a shovel made his head ache a little, so Eli did most of the digging. When the grave was filled in, they tossed the shovels aside, and they all stood around the grave.

Johnny said, "I wish my nephew Tom was here. He's a lawman now, but he was a minister for a lot of years. He'd know what to say here. What prayers to say."

Eli stood beside Missy. He said, "Mister Jones said once that God touches us by touching our heart, and when He touches our heart, we're touching His."

Johnny nodded. "I think maybe that's the greatest prayer of all."

They were silent a moment, each with their own thoughts.

Johnny didn't believe in looting, or in robbing from the dead, but there were six dead gunmen and he found no sign of identification on any of them. No letters addressed to them. One had a pocket watch and often folks engraved their initials on such things, but there was nothing on this one.

He knew Eli could use a pair of boots. He was in shoes that had a hole in the sole, and the leather was beginning to crack in places. Eli was tall for his age and one of the gunmen a little on the short side, so when Johnny and Eli were digging graves, Johnny pulled the boots from the corpse. He wiped them out and had Eli give them a try. They were a perfect fit.

"A man has to have boots," Johnny said.

He also took a pistol belt with cartridge loops in the back and had Eli try it on. The pistol was a Colt, and it seemed to fit Eli's hand well.

Johnny said, "You handled my old Remingtons well in that gunfight. I can tell Mister Jones taught you well. I'll keep on teaching you, if you'd like."

"You'd do that?"

Johnny nodded. "You're a good man, Eli. The way you handled yourself during that gun battle, when I was down—you saved Melissa Jean's life and you saved mine."

Eli decided it was time to fix the shoe on Thunder's front hoof.

"It looks a little loose," he said. "Not that he lets me check it. I try to, and he walks away from me."

Johnny chuckled. "That's Thunder."

"I can tell the shoe's bad by the way he walks. Don't know how it happened. It was that way when he brought you in. He wouldn't be able to carry a rider long without it getting sore."

"You know your horses," he said.

Eli nodded. "Yes, sir. I did a lot of farrier work and blacksmithin' back home. My daddy was teachin' me."

"Those are good trades to have. But shoeing Thunder is a different sort of thing. That horse is half-wild. There aren't many who can work with him."

"I'll give it a try. You still got to rest up from that concussion. But first we gotta find him. He must have jumped the fence again. I haven't seen him all day."

"He's not far," Johnny said. "He just doesn't like corrals. I saw him this morning, when I was out front with a cup of coffee. He was at the edge of the woods."

Johnny stepped back and let out a loud whistle. Then he waited. Then he let out another whistle.

"There he is," Eli said.

Thunder was trotting toward them, through the pines beyond the front of the cabin. Johnny could see it was clear Thunder was favoring his left front leg.

Johnny caught Thunder by the hackamore and said, "All right. Don't fight me."

Thunder shook his head a couple of times, but let Johnny lead him into the corral.

Eli said, "I can't believe he came when you whistled for him."

"He's the second horse I've had that does that."

Eli tried to get Thunder to lift his hoof. The way he tapped on the inside of the horse's leg told Johnny that Eli indeed knew what he was doing. But it didn't work with Thunder. The horse just pulled away from him, let out a loud snort, and flipped his head first one way and then the other.

Then Melissa Jean opened the gate and stepped in. She walked up to Thunder and said, "Easy, boy. He ain't gonna hurt you."

Thunder grew still as she walked up. She reached one hand gently under his chin, and with the other she began stroking his nose.

"I'll be danged," Johnny said. "I've seen only one other who could do that with him. My daughter Bree."

"Go ahead, Eli," she said. "He'll let you work on him, now."

Eli tapped Thunder's leg, and Thunder lifted his hoof.

Melissa Jean said, "I've always just had a way with animals."

Johnny leaned his elbows on the fence and watched Melissa Jean stroking Thunder's nose, while Eli hammered at the shoe.

Eli said, "He's got a small crack in the hoof wall. Whatever happened to make his shoe loose in the first place might have somethin' to do with it. Might have happened when he attacked that gunfighter too. I'm gonna make a bar shoe for him. Gotta fire up the forge."

Jeb had a small forge, not unlike the one back at the ranch. It would be good enough for a small job like this. Once Johnny was home, Thunder would get an extended vacation so his hoof could heal properly.

Johnny didn't have to ask if Eli really knew enough about smithing and farrier work to do the job. Something about Eli told Johnny that anything Eli did, he did well.

While Eli got the forge fired up, Melissa Jean kept Thunder calm, stroking his neck and talking in low, soothing tones. At one point, she wrapped her arms around Thunder's neck and snuggled him, and the horse actually leaned his head into her.

That was when Johnny had a thought. An idea about the future for both Melissa Jean and Eli. He didn't know if the kids would be game, and the family back home would have to go along with it. But the more he thought about it, the more it just felt right.

46

A week after the gunfight, Johnny was feeling steady and hadn't had a dizzy spell for a few days. Now that Thunder was ready to ride, Johnny decided to saddle him up and do a little scouting. Make sure there were no more riders out there looking for Eli and Melissa Jean.

Eli was in a flannel shirt with suspenders over his shoulders and linsey-woolsey pants. Johnny thought one of the first things he did, once they got back to the ranch, was buy Eli some canvas pants. He was wearing his boots like he was born to them. His gunbelt was in place and looked natural.

Johnny said, "I want you to keep watch while I'm gone. I should be back by nightfall."

"That shoe should serve Thunder fine," Eli said. "Just ride a little easy."

Johnny grinned. "Yes, sir."

He turned Thunder away from the cabin. A good rule of thumb was not to take the same route every time. The last time Jeb had ridden into camp, he had done so by riding straight in from the east. Johnny turned Thunder toward the cliff and rode south alongside a ridge, and then turned west.

He had a canteen with him, and his Sharps rifle was in the saddle boot. They had taken a couple of Winchesters from the dead gunmen, and Eli had them both at the cabin.

As Johnny rode, he would glance toward the trees and toward any points around him that might provide cover for an ambush. Old habits, he thought. He also looked at the ground for tracks. Any signs of riders.

The wound on his head was doing well. No sign of infection. The stitches Melissa Jean had put in were still there, and Johnny thought he would leave them until he got home. Granny Tate could remove them.

He saw occasional elk as he rode. At one point, he came across what looked like a game trail, and he followed it to a small stream. He stepped down from the saddle and let Thunder drink.

He decided to have a look at the hoof and tapped the back of the leg. Thunder looked at him but kept the hoof on the ground. Not everyone had the pleasure of inspecting Thunder's hooves. Johnny often had to do so by walking Thunder through some soft or muddy earth and then examining the tracks.

Their former wrangler, Fred Mitchum, had been one of the few who could change a shoe on Thunder. Dusty was allowed to, as long as Bree was there to coddle the horse, the way Melissa Jean had earlier. Now Eli had joined the club.

Johnny rode on. At one point, Thunder seemed to want to bear eastward through a small flat area. A ravine was to one side, and the beginning of a wooded ridge to the other. Johnny decided to let the horse have his head.

They traveled along. Thunder maintained a slow trot. Johnny often let the horse choose his own speed.

Thunder turned Johnny down a small slope that was sandy toward the bottom. Thunder held still and slid the last few feet.

Johnny thought he remembered this area, but he wasn't sure. He estimated Dillon was now only a few miles away.

Then he saw the body on the ground. He nudged Thunder forward.

You couldn't touch your spurs to Thunder. Johnny leaned forward and tapped his neck, and said, "Go ahead."

Thunder led him to the body. Johnny didn't have to tug on a rein at all to stop him. That's when Johnny realized Thunder had been bringing him to this spot.

The body had been here for a while, and animals had found it. It wasn't pretty. But then Johnny saw something curious. On the ground near the body was a hat that looked like his. The one he figured he had lost when he had been shot.

He swung out of the saddle and picked up the hat. It was his, all right. A little damp at the top of the crown, and one side of the brim was bent a little.

He pulled the hat down over his head, doing it easily, to make sure it didn't hurt his wound. The hat was old and the felt was soft, and it didn't aggravate the wound at all.

He looked at the body. He remembered little about that day, and didn't remember being shot at all.

He looked at the body, the way it was dressed. Tall, black riding boots that rose to the knee. Tan, canvas pants. A gray range shirt. The shirt had been torn by critters. Coyotes, buzzards, whatever. The gunbelt was worn, black leather.

The outfit looked familiar. Then Johnny realized where he had seen it before. He was certain Reno had been wearing clothes like this. Gray shirt, tan pants, black leather riding boots. His pantlegs had been tucked in, old-style. He thought Reno's gunbelt had been black leather.

The man had been big. Taller than Johnny and heavily muscled. There was also some fat, the way strong men sometimes get fat as their youth deserts them. Reno had certainly been a big man.

Could this be Reno? he asked himself. Could Reno have taken a shot at him?

Johnny looked at Thunder, the full realization dawning on him.

He said to the horse, "This is Reno, isn't it? He shot me and then came down from wherever he was hiding to finish off the job. And you killed him. That's how you hurt your hoof."

The horse didn't react. Johnny didn't really expect him to. But saying the words out loud helped him to organize his thoughts.

He found it a little difficult to believe that Reno would do something like that. Shoot him from behind.

And yet, there had always been a little back-stabbing streak in Reno, especially when there was liquor in him.

Johnny walked over to Thunder. He didn't touch the horse's nose. Only Bree could get away with that. And now Melissa Jean. Instead he patted the horse on the side of the neck a couple of times.

Johnny said, "You're one heck of a horse, you know that?"

Something about the look in Thunder's eyes, Johnny thought he knew it.

47

Johnny was back at the cabin not much before evening. Melissa Jean had supper on the stove, and Eli was chopping firewood.

Johnny said to Eli, "I rode far and wide. Didn't see any sign of riders at all. But I did find the remains of the man who I think tried to kill me. And I found my hat."

Over supper, Johnny told them about Reno. What kind of man he had been, and the encounter they had in the saloon in Dillon.

"I'm feeling a lot better now," Johnny said. "Riding didn't bother me at all. I should probably be riding on. It's too late to make the cattle auction in Idaho, so I'll just head home. I have a family waiting for me, back in Montana."

Johnny took a sip of coffee. "Have you two given any thought about the future?"

Melissa Jean shrugged. "I don't know where we'll go."

Eli said, "We got nobody but each other. I was figuring maybe we could stay on here at the cabin. Mister Jones was showing me how to hunt, and I can shoot. We can grow crops. Missy can take care of the cabin."

She gave Eli a look, and said, "Melissa Jean."

Johnny nodded. "I'm sure you two could do fairly well here, but I've been putting a lot of thought to something. I promised Mister Jones I'd look after you. I can't just ride off and leave the two of you here. But I can't really stay, either, because my family is missing me, I'm sure, and they need me."

He looked at them both. He said, "Seems like I have a dilemma doesn't it?"

Eli said, "You really don't have to worry about us. We'll be all right."

"But what about that mean old aunt you talk

about? What if she sends more men looking for you?"

Melissa Jean said, "Maybe they won't find the cabin."

Johnny shrugged. "That group of men we fought found the cabin. Others could."

"What do you suggest?"

"I think you should come back to the ranch with me, to our little valley. We'll figure out the rest once we're there."

Eli said, "We don't like to accept charity."

Johnny shook his head. "It won't be charity. I doubt you two would ever have a problem pulling your own weight. And besides, you took me in. Helped me. It wouldn't be right for me to just ride on and leave you here. And I made that promise to Mister Jones. You wouldn't want me to go back on my word, would you?"

Melissa Jean looked at Eli with a smile. "We couldn't ask him to go back on his word, could we?"

Eli was smiling too. "No, ma'am."

Melissa Jean said, "We'll come back with you. When do you want us all to leave?"

Johnny said, "I was thinking about the morning. It's a two-day ride. We'll be staying over once, camping in the mountains."

Come morning, Eli and Johnny saddled Thunder, Eli's horse, and the horse that had been Jeb's. Johnny's saddle bags were stuffed with a sack of flour and the can of Arbuckle coffee, and his soogan was tied to the back. They used blankets from the cabin to make soogans for Eli and Melissa Jean.

They had found the six horses that had belonged to the men who had attacked the cabin.

Eli said, "Should we bring them along? Maybe one or two of them could serve as pack horses."

Johnny shook his head. "Won't need packhorses. I always travel with only what I can carry on Thunder. We'll shoot our supper tonight."

Eli nodded. He liked the sound of that.

They turned the horses free and left the saddles in the small barn. They did keep a couple of the canteens, and two additional sets of saddlebags.

In one saddlebag was a bottle of whiskey. Johnny pulled the plug and emptied it onto the ground.

"I used to drink too much of this," Johnny said. "Got me into trouble when I was younger. Now I mostly leave it alone."

Melissa Jean was in an old pair of britches she had found in the cabin. A girl can't very well ride in a full skirt.

She swung up in the saddle and sat there looking like she belonged on the back of a horse. Johnny figured he shouldn't be surprised.

She looked at the cabin. "I'm going to miss this little place. It was home for us for a year."

Eli grinned at her. "Your father always said you were the sentimental one, Missy."

She gave him a look. "Melissa Jean."

Johnny said, "You know, *Melissa Jean* is kind of a mouthful."

"But Missy is what they called me when I was a child. I'm growed now. I should have a growed-up name."

Johnny thought about it for a moment. "How about M.J.?"

She looked thoughtful, tossing that idea around in her head. "I think I could live with that."

Johnny climbed up onto Thunder's back and gave one last look to the little cabin. The roof sagged a little on one side. No glass in the windows and no foundation. A sorry-looking little place, he thought. Yet, so much had happened here, and they were leaving a good man in a grave out front.

Eli had made a cross and pounded it into the earth at the head of the grave. They didn't know how old Jeb was or even what his full name was, so with a poker hot from the stove, Eli burned the words,

JEB JONES.
D. 1882.
GIVED HIS LIFE FOR US ALL.

Johnny couldn't think of a better sentiment to have people remember you by.

48

They didn't hurry traveling through the mountains. Partly because of Thunder's hoof and partly because, even though Johnny was feeling better, he didn't want to push it.

They spent two nights in the mountains. Johnny shot a deer with his Sharps rifle, and they roasted venison on a wooden spit Johnny carved with a bowie knife.

They spread their bedrolls on the ground near the fire and Melissa Jean looked out at the darkness, beyond the edge of the firelight.

"It's dark out there," she said.

A wolf howled, from somewhere off in the distance. Then three more picked up the tune.

"They're a long way off," Johnny said. "Look at Thunder over there. He doesn't look nervous."

Johnny had picketed the horses a short ways from the campfire. Except for Thunder. The horse didn't like to be picketed or hobbled, so Johnny let him run free. Thunder was now nosing the grass fifteen feet from the fire.

She said, "I doubt there's much that makes that horse nervous. But I'm not him."

Eli was adding more wood to the fire. His Colt revolver was holstered at his right hip, and his Winchester was on his blankets.

He said, "Don't worry, M.J. Mister McCabe and I won't let nothin' happen to you."

She grinned. "M.J., huh?"

He nodded. "I think it's a good idea. I might take to callin' you Emmy for short."

"You'd better not."

As Johnny listened, he couldn't help but grin. Brother and sister, he thought. You don't need to be blood-related to be family.

It was a little before noon on their third day in the saddle that they rode across the wooden bridge and up to the ranch house.

Jessica gave him a longer hug than he had expected.

"I'm just so glad you're home," she said. "I had such a bad feeling about this trip."

"I had quite an adventure, all right. I'll tell you all about it."

Haley looked at Johnny's wound and removed the stitches.

"I'm really sorry to hear about Granny Tate," Johnny said. "She's gonna be missed. But I think you're gonna do a fine job in her place."

"I hope so," she said. "There's so much I need to learn."

"There always is. And the more you learn, the more you realize you need to learn."

She grinned. "Shoshone wisdom?"

He shook his head. "Mister Chen said it once, a long time ago."

She held up one finger and moved it back and forth, and told him to follow it with his eyes without moving his head. He had no idea why, but he had seen Granny Tate do it once, when Zack had his concussion.

"I think you're gonna be fine," she said.

"I figured. My head's too hard to be otherwise."

Johnny greeted Scott Hansen with a handshake.

"Hansen," Johnny said. "How many years has it been?"

"The Gunman of the Rio Grande," Scott said.

Bree was laughing. "Don't call him that. He hates it."

Scott was grinning. "He hated it back then too."

Over supper, Josh and Dusty told their pa about the range war with the Willburys.

"I'm sorry to hear about that," Johnny said. "Tom

Willbury was a good man. I don't like the idea of bad blood between our families."

Come evening, Jessica got the twins to sleep upstairs and then came down for a few minutes.

"I don't like leaving them alone for long," she said.

Cora was asleep. Dusty, Haley and Jonathan were still at the house, and Jonathan was asleep in the bed Johnny and Jessica were using while they were at the house.

There was limited space upstairs, so Eli volunteered to sleep in the bunkhouse, but Johnny wouldn't hear of it. He and M.J. were in their bedrolls, on the floor in Johnny and Jessica's room.

"They're exhausted," Johnny said, coming downstairs. "Those two have been through a lot."

The chair Johnny had always taken by the stone hearth was now out at the cabin he shared with Jessica and Cora, and Josh had put a chair of his own there. But it was in the same place Johnny's chair had been, so Josh insisted that Johnny take it for the evening. Temperence gave up her rocker to Aunt Ginny, so for this evening, Johnny and Aunt Ginny were in their old places.

Josh got a carafe from the desk, poured some glasses of scotch, and handed one to Johnny.

Charles was upstairs asleep. He had lost a lot of blood and it would be a while before he was at full strength. Bree was in the parlor, sitting with her back to the fire, a glass of wine in one hand.

Sam was standing, leaning one hand against the wooden mantel, and he had a glass of scotch. He was in a tie and jacket. It seemed to Johnny the man was always dressed like a riverboat gambler, like he had been when Johnny met him back in California, nigh onto three years ago. Again, old habits die hard, he supposed.

"There's something I want to tell you all about those two," Johnny said. "Eli and M.J."

Over supper, he had told them about his

adventures with them. But now he talked about it all in greater detail. The shooting Eli had done, when the man had broken in through the front door. The shooting he had done to take out the final gunman. And how he worked hard, and yet efficiently. All of the various skills the boy had.

"He's only twelve," Johnny said, "but I hate to call him a boy. He's more of a man than a lot of men I know."

Johnny told them about M.J, and about her heart and courage. How she could be sweet and yet tough as steel. And he told them about how she was with Thunder.

"Looks like I have a kindred spirit," Bree said.

Johnny talked about their background in Alabama, about how they had no living family, except for the aunt who was chasing after them. He talked about how Eli didn't even have a last name. Not a real one.

"John," Ginny said, "you're leading somewhere with all of this."

Johnny nodded. He said "I don't ask this lightly, but I want to bring them into the family. Lock, stock and barrel. I want them to be McCabes."

He looked at Dusty, who nodded, and then to Jack, who was seated with Nina in chairs they had brought in from the kitchen.

Johnny said, "We should all vote on it. Because I'm asking a lot."

"No you're not," Aunt Ginny said. "Those children belong here."

Johnny looked at Jessica. He had told her about this earlier, when they had some time upstairs while she was nursing the twins.

She said, "You already have my vote. I agree with Aunt Ginny."

Josh said, "Pa, I think it's unanimous to say..,"

Temperence finished it for him, "Absolutely, yes. You welcomed me into this family when I had nowhere to go."

Dusty said, "It seems like what we do."

Aunt Ginny smiled. "Yes, indeed. It surely does."

49

The following morning, Temperence had steak and eggs on the stove. Johnny so liked this girl's cooking.

He sat at the head of table—a place he felt should go to Josh now, but Josh had insisted Johnny take it. Johnny had a steak and some scrambled eggs in front of him and a cup of trail coffee.

Jessica was upstairs with the twins, but Cora was downstairs and at the table. Charles was there, too, with his arm in a sling and Bree by his side.

Haley and Jonathan had gone home, but Dusty had ridden back out to the main house like he did every morning. He and Josh would be riding out to the herd. Roundup was over, but Josh wanted another look at the Twin Sisters country, just to make sure nothing new was developing.

"I've got a feeling things are far from over with Eugenia," he said.

It was while they ate that Johnny told M.J. and Eli about what the family had discussed the night before.

"You have a place in this family, if you want it," Johnny said. "You'll both live with Jessica and me, out in our canyon. Eli, you'll work here at the ranch."

He said, "You mean, like a real cowhand?"

Josh said, "Not *like* a real cowhand. You'll *be* a real cowhand."

"You'll have a lot to learn," Johnny said, "but I think you're up to it."

"And me," M.J. said, "what'll I do?"

"Work with Jessica. Help her keep house. Help her and Cora with the twins."

Cora said, "You mean, M.J. will be my sister?"

Johnny nodded. "If that's what M.J. wants."

M.J. looked at Eli. Johnny figured it was all a little overwhelming.

Johnny said, "Jessica and I would never try to replace the parents of either of you. But we can be like a second mother and father, if you'd let us."

"You mean," Eli said, "I'd be like your son?"

"That's exactly what I mean."

"But, I'm colored."

"In this family," Aunt Ginny said, "that makes no difference."

Johnny said, "A wise man said to me once that there really is no white or colored. Those are just labels people made up. We're all children of God and equal in His eyes."

He took a sip of coffee, and began sawing into his steak. "When you live on the frontier, you learn real quick that what really matters is a man or a woman's heart. Their honesty. How hard they work. If they have courage. Color doesn't mean a thing."

Ginny said, "My father was a sea captain, and he learned similar lessons out to sea."

"But here on the frontier, we find that as civilization works its way in, a lot of the foolish notions from people in more so-called civilized parts come with them. But not in this family."

Dusty said, "Eli, I know what it's like not to have a name. I didn't, for a long time. But the McCabe name is a good one, and it's yours if you want it."

Eli looked at M.J., and she nodded.

He said to Johnny, "Mister McCabe, M.J. and I would like to accept your offer."

"One condition, though. You don't call me Mister McCabe. You call me Pa." He looked at M.J. "That goes for both of you."

She gave a big smile. "I think we can manage that, Pa."

50

Johnny and Jessica were in bed, and her head was against his shoulder. The night air was cool, and the covers were pulled to their chins.

They were in their cabin at the edge of their little canyon.

"It's so good to have you back," Jessica said.

With one hand, he was playing with her hair.

He said, "I know I'm asking a lot of the family, to welcome in two kids they hardly know."

She shook her head. "I always believed you can tell a lot about a person by the look in their eyes. Those are two good kids."

The twins were in their cribs, by the foot of the bed. Cora was in her room, sharing her bed with M.J., and Eli was sleeping in blankets on the floor by the fireplace.

Johnny said, "Eli and I'll get started in the morning, adding on the new bedrooms. Once the new rooms are done, Eli can start working with Josh and Dusty."

"I suppose we're going to get some grief from people in town for having a colored boy in the family."

Johnny shrugged. "Let them give us grief. I'll give it right back to them."

She grinned. "I could expect nothing less from a McCabe."

"So, you certainly have a houseful now."

"And I love it. It wasn't that long ago that it was just Cora and me. Now we have not only the twins, but two more. And I have the man of my dreams."

Johnny said, "Man of your dreams. I like that title."

She laughed and said, "Don't let it go to your head now."

"Go to my head?"

She had a ticklish spot on her ribs and Johnny found it. She yelped and squirmed away, but then he pulled her back.

She said, "I was afraid, you know. Something about this time, when you left. I was truly afraid something would happen to you, and you wouldn't come back. And you almost didn't. If the bullet shot by that man Reno had been just a little more true, you wouldn't be here."

Johnny said, "I've been giving that some thought. I think my days of traveling overland are done. Civilization is coming. Looks like the railroad will be in Jubilee by next year. I think my long adventures are going to be done. From now on, if I have to go somewhere, I'll buy a train ticket. I don't want you to have to be afraid, anymore."

She snuggled back into him. "I think I'm going to like that."

Then they were quiet, and she drifted off to sleep on his shoulder.

Johnny listened to the sound of her breathing. Beyond the foot of the bed, one of the babies made a cooing sound in its sleep. The ceiling creaked a bit, and from somewhere out in the night, a wolf called out to the moon.

A Note From The Author

I hope you all enjoyed this novel. If you want to drop me an email, I can be reached at mccabewesterns@gmail.com. I'm also on Facebook.

In this novel, some gunfighters are mentioned who are actually characters in novels written by other writers. I believe it's good for writers not to compete against each other, but to work together for the greater enjoyment of our readers. I like to think that that all of these characters exist in the same fictional world. The copyright to novels the following characters appear in belongs to each respective author.

Robert "Gray Eagle" McAllister appears in the novel *Death of an Eagle,* by Kirby Jonas. Kirby has a number of westerns under his belt, as well as novels from other genres. His books can be found on Amazon, and they are well worth the read.

Bass Reeves appears in *The Nations* series by Ken Farmer and Buck Steinke. This character is based on an actual lawman from the Old West. Ken and Buck each have a background in movies and TV, as well as the military. Ken is an accomplished horseman and Buck knows just about everything there is to know about guns and ballistics. The Nations novels are available on Amazon.

Shad Cain appears in novels by Lou Bradshaw. Lou has a whole bunch of western novels available on Amazon featuring Cain, as well as Ben Blue and J.L. Tate. Lou also has a novel called *A Fine Kettle of Fish,* which is not a western, but falls into the genre usually called "serious fiction." Despite the name of the genre, this novel is outright funny and a great read.

Jim Austin is my own character, and will be appearing in a series called *The Austins* that began with an idea I put together with my father, many years ago. Jeb Jones also appears in the series. I hope to have the first novel out next year.

Luke Baker is also my own. He will be appearing in an upcoming series of mine called *Baker Canyon*. A goal I had when I was younger was to create and produce a TV series, so in light of that, I am writing *Baker Canyon* as a series of novellas, each one paced like a TV episode. The first four will be released all at the same time, probably sometime in 2017.

Brad Dennison
Buford, Georgia
October, 2016